BLURB

Now that she's mine, I'm never letting her go.

If only she would let me protect her. Seeing the fear in her eyes makes me want to do the one thing I've vowed never to do again... kill.

But I'll do anything to protect what's mine.

The finale of The Force Duet. Must be read AFTER the first book, Force.

ENFORCE

M. MALONE
NANA MALONE

CONTENTS

- The Shameless Trilogy -

Shame (prequel)

Shameless / Shameful / UnAshamed

- The Force Duet -

Forcful (prequel)

Force / Enforce

- The Deep Duet -

In Deep (prequel)

Deep / Deeper

- The Sin Duet -

Beyond Sin (prequel)

Sin / Sinful

ENFORCE

umb terror.

That's all JJ felt. She was so angry and worried and sick she couldn't even move, breathe, or speak. Someone had taken Isabella right from her home. "This is all my fault. It had to have been David."

Jonas rubbed her back in slow circles. "This has nothing to do with you. This has to do with *us*. All of us. They want a war, they've got one."

JJ turned into Jonas's arms and her gaze flickered up to his. "I wish it was that simple. You don't understand. *This* is what he does. He terrorizes everyone around you so that you're completely alone. So that no one will want to be with you. So that you're a pariah. I wish I could say he's the kind of man who wouldn't hurt a baby just to fuck with me. But he would."

Jonas held her tight. "We're not going to let that happen. I promise. We're going to get Isabella back."

A sob racked her body. What was she supposed to do? How was she supposed to fix this? She had brought pain to her friends. Into her family. Once her parents moved away to Florida to be closer to their friends, she had no one else. These guys were the only family she had. And because of her, Noah and Lucia's baby was gone.

From the couch Matthias groaned, and Noah ran to him. "Kid?" Noah shook him hard and slapped his face. "Kid, wake up."

Matthias groaned some more, and even in his sluggish, obviously drugged state, he managed to defend against some of Noah's assaults. JJ was pretty sure she would've just lain there like a rag.

When Noah slapped him again, Matthias caught his arm, cranked it under his own, and then raised his other hand to hit him in the face. But then he blinked rapidly and realized who he was about to hit and released Noah. "Blimey. Pretty sure the fucking twat drugged me. What the fuck?" He tried to sit up, but Noah shoved him back down.

"Easy. We don't know what she gave you yet. Doc's on his way to take your blood and will rush some lab results."

Matthias shook him off. "I'm all right. Just a fucking bitch of a headache." And then he let out a slew of curses that JJ could only assume came from a lifetime rolling about the streets of London. When he pushed himself into a sitting position, Lucia went to him and kneeled in front of him, holding his hands.

"Matthias, do you remember anything? Anything at all? They took Isabella."

Matthias's brows snapped down and he stared at Lucia hard. "The baby? Fucking cunt took the baby?"

His gaze darted to Noah whose expression was grim and his jaw set. But he nodded. "Yeah, they took the babysitter too."

Matthias shook his head, and then groaned loudly as he cradled it gently with both hands. "Nah, mate, no one took her. She brought me a drink. Said she made tea. Fucking Earl Grey. I was downed because I wanted a spot of tea. That is so fucking bullshit."

Lucia shook her head. "But I vetted Katie. *You* vetted Katie. We all did."

It was true. The nanny had been interviewed by every single member of Blake Security. They'd dug through her background, her past boyfriends, any roommates she had. They'd gone over her financial records. That babysitter pretty much had top-secret clearance at this point with all the background checks she'd had.

"I know." Matthias said. "But it was her. No one else could've accessed or bypassed the biometric scanner or the alarms. Unless those were on when you guys came in."

Next to JJ, Jonas stiffened. "No. No alarms. Our phones didn't go off either. Nothing."

Matthias cursed again. "Yeah. It was Katie then because no one else could have gotten in here."

"Kid, you feeling up to it? We need to access the security feed to see what happened, and you're the only one who can do that quickly," Noah said.

"Fuck. You've been waiting for me to wake up? We're losing time." He pushed to his feet and swayed, and Noah shoved him back down into a sitting position. "You stay here. Oskar, run and bring the kid his laptop."

JJ had never seen the German run so fast. But he was back in less than a minute and handed the laptop to Matthias. Matthias's fingers tapped over the keyboard at such a fast rate she could barely see the individual strokes he was making. "Yeah, mate. Here she is; bloody cunt is in the kitchen making the tea." He turned the laptop around, but when they all couldn't see it he made another few quick taps, and the security footage appeared on the television set. He pointed. "Yeah, there she is, putting whatever it is in the tea. And then she brings it in here to me. I was working on something. But Isabella refused to sleep, so I had her one-handed, you know. Like you do sometimes, Noah, so that she can see outward and play a little, and then she falls asleep."

Noah's lips twitched, and he blinked back tears. "Yeah, I know."

Matthias sniffed too. "Fuck mate. I'm so fucking sorry. I'm such a fucking idiot. I took the tea. I drank it. Didn't taste any different, didn't smell any different."

Noah shook his head. "This isn't on you. This is on her. We just need to see the rest of the video."

Matthias fast-forwarded the video to show what happened when his head started to nod back. Katie took the baby, and then she made one call. "Yes. He's out." She was silent for a beat, and then her gaze darted to Matthias and back to the baby. "I don't think I can do that. If that's what you want to happen, you'll have to come and do it yourself. Because I won't. I told you that already."

"Is there any way we can track who she was talking to?" Jonas asked.

Matthias frowned. "I might be able to hack her phone. Pinpoint her location. Read her text messages. But without the actual physical phone, it will be next to impossible to determine who she called. I'm fucking sorry. This is on me."

JJ stepped out of the comfort of Jonas's arms. "No Matthias. I've already taken the blame. It's because of me that all of you are in this position. He wants me. That's why he took her. Because he knows it would hurt me to see all of you hurting. Matthias this wasn't your fault. We'll find Katie. If anyone can do it, you can."

Lucia nodded. "JJ's right. You would be the one who could find her."

"I'll do my best. Again, I'm so fucking sorry."

"Don't be sorry. This wasn't you. Just find her," Noah said.

Lucia stood and turned to JJ. "Look, I know you blame yourself, JJ. I actually blame myself for leaving. I know Noah's gonna rip himself apart. And Matthias, you're killing yourself because you drank tea. None of us are to blame. The person to blame is this Chamaeleon character. He and Katie. We blame *them*. And now we all have to band together and bring my daughter home."

Noah wrapped his arms around her. "Lucia's right. We are a family. We won't crumble. And together, we're going to find my daughter. Even if it means taking the fight straight to ORUS. We *will* get her back."

Matthias tried to stand again but thought better of it. "That's just the thing you guys. I'm not entirely sure ORUS is behind this."

Calm, he had to stay fucking calm. Jonas dragged in a deep breath in hopes that one breath would keep him from wanting to pull something apart. He was going to kill that fucker. And he was going to take his time. And he was going to enjoy it.

There's plenty of time for killing him later.

They had to catch him first. And as much as he wanted to kill the asshole right now, his priority was JJ. He could almost feel her shaking as she stood next to him.

"Babe, want to take Lucia into the kitchen? Make her some tea, see what you can do to help her. I'll talk to Matthias and see what we can seam together about the sequence of events, okay?"

The JJ he knew would argue about why she needed to be in the room with them when they were discussing things and vowing to kill the fucker herself. But that part of her was in shock. Instead, she simply nodded, went to her best friend, took her hand, and led her through the expansive living area to the back hallway and into the kitchen.

Jonas could only stare after her as she left the room. Would this be the thing that broke her? How the hell did he help her fix this? *She'll be okay. She's strong. Right now, someone else needs your support.*

He turned his attention to Noah and winced when he saw the fear in his friend's eyes. Noah's lips were thin, his gaze bleak. What hell he must be going through right now. Jonas stepped toward his friend, but Noah jutted out his chin. "Let's get to work. Matthias, are you able to get into our back up security feed?"

From the couch, the kid nodded and tried to get himself up. The kid was too weak though, so Oskar and Rafe helped him to his feet. He was so unsteady, they half-dragged him into the hallway and back into his domain. Once they had him seated in his usual post, he sagged into his seat.

He had to give the kid credit, because as shitty as he must feel, he was still ready to work.

"All right gents, I know it's an easy thing to jump to conclusions about who's responsible for this, but I've had eyes on Chamaeleon since the other day. He hasn't moved. Not once, in or out, at least according to my feeds. I've also had eyes on ORUS headquarters just in case he found a way around my protocols. It's easy to assume it's him. But," he shook his head. "According to this, the guy's an agoraphobic or something. He hasn't left his flat."

Noah rubbed the stubble on his jaw. "How many exits are there in that building?"

"There are four. I have cameras on all of them."

Jonas wracked his brain. "This guy is good at hiding. I

mean that's pretty much what they trained him for. We have to be missing something."

Matthias shook his head. "No. His door hasn't even opened. Two days, and he's been holed up in that flat. Unless he sprouted wings and flew."

Jonah scowled. "I mean, that's possible, right?"

"I appreciate the confidence in the skill set, Jonas, but even ORUS agents can't fly."

"No, but they can rappel and shit, right Rafe?"

Lucia's brother nodded. "That's a possibility. I've done it. But as a means of getting in and out of a building, it's risky. Someone is bound to see you. But if the building has a basement or connects to a tunnel, it's a good way in and out."

Noah spoke, his voice low and gravelly. Like every word was painfully wrenched out of him. "Matthias, start looking at building plans of what was there before this apartment complex. Then start looking for any connection between David West and Katie. Anything at all. In the meantime, I'll send Dylan to her apartment. Though it's doubtful she's there, he might find something that leads us to her. And let's have Ryan start canvasing her known haunts. Everywhere she's been known to go. I want her credit card numbers. I want her phone number. Hell I want her library card number. Anything that can help find my daughter."

Matthias and Dylan gave him curt nods.

"Noah," the kid swallowed hard. "Really fucking sorry."

Noah visibly shook. "This isn't on you. This is on that woman and Chamaeleon. All we can do is what we all do best."

Jonas studied Noah and wondered if his friend, Matthias, and Rafe would be coming out of assassin retirement to handle this guy. And if they were coming out of retirement did that mean that Katie was fair game too?

Noah hadn't ever given him full details of what he'd done for ORUS, but Jonas been able to piece together enough. The three of them, they had killed before. A lot. The part of him that was still a cop bristled at that. But he knew better than anyone there were times when extreme measures were called for. This was one of those times. And if there was killing to be done for the bastard who took Isabella, well then count him in.

"Matthias, walk us through what happened from the

moment we left. Just one more time. Show us everything," Noah said.

Jonas turned his attention to Noah. "Listen, I know you're going to tell me no. But why don't you let me handle this? Because right now you're too raw, and you're in shock. You and I both know you're not at your best right now. Not to mention the cops will be here any second. You're about to have your hands full. Let me do this."

Noah's shake of the head was automatic. "She's my daughter. *I'll* do this."

"You can't do *this* and deal with the cops. Go." Even as he spoke, the buzzer indicated someone was downstairs. "See, the police are already here. You deal with them and the official channels. Maybe this *is* a simple case of the babysitter going crazy. If it is, we'll find her in no time. If it isn't, the kid will work with the team. We have it under control."

Noah looked like he was going to refuse again. But when Dylan poked his head into the computer room and nodded at him, indicating the cops were there, he really had no choice. When he finally nodded, Jonas could see the sag in his body. He could see his friend giving up the fight.

When Noah shuffled out of the room to deal with the police, Jonas turned his attention back to Matthias and Rafe and assumed command. Rafe might be back in the fold, but Jonas had the most seniority on this team.

"Okay, it's just us." To Matthias, he said, "How are you holding up?"

The kid flattened his lips. "Yeah, mate, I'm good. Now let's catch this cunt."

CHAPTER TWO

JJ stood at the periphery of the room, watching as everyone moved with purpose. Noah was on the warpath, his phone to his ear while simultaneously looking over Matthias's shoulder. Jonas and Oskar were conferring about something in somber tones across the room, both with expressions of grave worry.

It reminded her of the way things were the previous year when Lucia had been the one in hot water. They hadn't known at the time that her "stalker" was actually her brother, Rafe, so the guys had been in super-protective mode then, trying to keep someone on Lucia's protection detail at all times. Noah would have probably locked her in the penthouse back then if he could have gotten away with it. They'd still been fighting the inevitable back then, but JJ was sure her friend wouldn't have minded being locked away with Noah *too* much.

Her eyes swung to where her friend was sitting alone on the couch. She and Lucia had gone into the kitchen to make tea, but once they'd come back, the tea sat on the side table, forgotten as her friend stared into space. Every few moments, her fingers would twitch as if searching for the baby that should have been in her arms.

JJ shuddered. She wanted to go to Lucia, hug her and tell her it would all be okay. That was what she should have been doing as her best friend. But she couldn't seem to get her feet to move.

What right did she have to comfort Lucia? It was her fault her friend's daughter was missing.

"It's not your fault." Jonas's voice interrupted her thoughts.

JJ nodded because she knew that was what he expected, not because she agreed.

Jonas swore softly when she looked directly at him. "You're crying. Come here, baby."

She walked into his embrace and buried her face into his

shirt. He smelled like amber, something slightly smoky, and... home. JJ wasn't sure when it had happened exactly, but Jonas had become her safe place.

"It's rare that you cry," Jonas whispered. "I don't like it. I wish I could take the pain away."

She smiled tremulously. "No one can take this away. Not until Isabella is back where she belongs."

Inside, her mind was a muddle of guilt, confusion, and anger. What was David doing? It was like looking at a puzzle that had half the pieces missing. In the beginning, she'd assumed this whole thing was about showing her he was still around and could show up whenever he wanted. It was about control. David had always been so jealous and controlling, terrorizing her as she went about her life fit the profile of his previous methods perfectly.

But this? Taking an innocent child? This was something else entirely.

"We're pulling up security and traffic cams in the area to see if we can catch where Katie was going or if she met up with anyone." Jonas glanced over his shoulder to where Matthias was talking to Noah. "There's nowhere she can hide in this city. Noah has too many contacts."

JJ closed her eyes. "She's not the one I'm worried about."

Jonas sighed. "You still think it was Chamaeleon."

She shrugged. There was no use insisting when the evidence seemed so flimsy. It was more a gut feeling than anything else.

The whole time they'd been dating, he was careful to keep his abuse private. He'd only hit her places where no one would see the bruises. He'd been jealous of her attention to other men, but he'd played the affable, easygoing boyfriend in public, only to show her his rage as soon as they were behind closed doors. There had been only one occasion where he'd lost his temper where anyone else could see. He'd been careful to keep their dynamic away from other people, so why would he suddenly target Lucia's baby? She'd never even introduced him to Lucia back then. Her friend had been mourning her brother's death and hadn't been going out much at all.

"JJ, look at me. You are not to blame here."

"He's right. You should listen to him." Lucia's voice came from behind Jonas. They both turned to look at her.

Lucia's gray eyes were shadowed and slightly red from unshed tears. It hurt JJ just to look at her.

As usual, Jonas could sense her emotions. He pulled JJ closer and kissed her forehead. "Lucia loves you. We all do. Remember that. I'll leave you two to talk."

She watched as he hugged Lucia before walking over to join Noah and Matthias. When she looked back to Lucia, her friend watched her with knowing eyes.

"You can't fool me, Jessica Jones. We've known each other too long for that."

The use of her full name pulled a reluctant smile from JJ. Lucia only pulled out the big guns when she was serious.

"I'm not trying to fool you. I'm just ashamed."

"Why would you be ashamed? You've been nothing but a loving, protective godmother to Isabella. And I have no doubt that if you'd been here when it happened you'd have kicked that babysitter's ass. But you weren't here, and neither was I. Blaming ourselves for not being here doesn't get my daughter back. I don't need you to distance yourself because you feel guilty. I need my best friend to hold my hand so I don't lose my mind."

JJ held open her arms immediately. Lucia practically threw herself forward, holding on to her like a lifeline. She'd been keeping herself so busy with guilt and second thoughts that she hadn't realized she was also punishing Lucia.

"I'm so sorry. I didn't think you'd want to look at me knowing that I might have brought this danger on us."

Lucia wiped her eyes with the back of her hand. "Even if it is this Chamaeleon guy, do you think I blame you for the actions of that psycho? You're my sister, JJ. I couldn't love you any more if we were blood."

JJ blew out a breath as her own eyes welled with tears. "Oh hell, now you've got me crying too."

After a few minutes hugging it out, Lucia grabbed her hand and led her to the couch. JJ curled up on one side while Lucia took the other and they turned so their feet met in the middle. This was how they'd always sat together, starting from when they were teenagers. The familiar pose was a bit of comfort in the middle of chaos.

Lucia glanced behind them where the guys were talking. "Noah is going crazy. If I thought he was over protective where I'm concerned, he's way worse with Isabella. Whoever took her might as well pick out their gravestone." Her voice wavered slightly at the end.

JJ held out a hand and squeezed when Lucia took it. She

could hear what her friend was pointedly *not* saying. Her deepest fear. That even though Noah would tear the city apart to find their daughter, there was no guarantee Isabella would still be alive by the time he found her.

"Matthias can find anyone. I'm sure he can find whoever did this."

Lucia's eyes swung over to hers. "You really think David would do this to get back at you? It seems so strange. It would make more sense if Izzy were your baby."

"Maybe not. I'm probably wrong, and it's some random person that Noah and the guys helped put in jail in the past or something."

JJ closed her eyes and wished with her whole heart that could be true. Because if it was David, it meant his obsession with her was even bigger than she could have ever known. It also meant they wouldn't find Isabella until he wanted them to.

After all, David had never lacked patience. He'd waited over seven years to come back and take his revenge.

———

The next few days were some of the longest of JJ's life.

Noah didn't appear to have slept the entire time and neither had Lucia, if she took a guess. Every night her friend went into her room, but she came out the next day with the bags under her eyes deeper and darker. Not that JJ didn't understand. She'd brought work home with her but it hadn't taken her mind off things a bit. Her sleep had been filled with nightmares of David holding the baby just out of reach and drawing on her face with lipstick.

She'd woken in a cold sweat after that one.

One morning while sitting at the kitchen counter, she heard a commotion coming from down the hall. Noise was a part of life when living with so many men, but this was different. JJ abandoned her coffee cup and walked toward the sound. It was coming from Matthias's room.

She hadn't been in his room many times, but she remembered that it was taken up by a lot of screens and there were always a bunch of laptops lying around. As she got closer, she slowed her steps so the guys wouldn't hear her.

"I can't believe you found him."

That sounded like Jonas's voice. JJ inched a little closer. They'd all avoided speaking about the search for the missing babysitter in front of Lucia, so she'd only gotten a few updates from Jonas.

"It wasn't easy, mate. He's definitely one of us."

One of us? What did that mean? JJ shook her head. Lucia had hinted about Noah, Matthias, and Rafe sharing some sort of shady background, but she didn't know too much about it. Did that mean that David knew them? Maybe Jonas was right and this really wasn't about her. The sound of Matthias's laugh brought her back to the present conversation.

"Bloody wanker. He actually thought he could proxy off some server in Russia for his emails to throw me off his scent. Like I'm some amateur."

Jonas's deep laugh came next. "Not sure what the fuck you just said, but I assume that means you know where he is?"

"Yeah, he's still in New York. Fucker got an apartment in the East Village on 10th like it was nothing. He's clearly not worried about us finding him. Not sure why he's still hanging around if he doesn't want to be caught."

JJ's mind immediately started spinning. She put a hand over her mouth, sure that she'd scream or cry or something and give away that she was listening. But there was only one reason David would hang around New York instead of hiding out.

Her.

"Look, I think it's best if we keep this quiet for now. The girls are already on edge. So let's not mention anything until we know more." Jonas's voice brought her out of her daze.

It was just like him to want to spare them more pain. She thought of Lucia and her haunted eyes. She didn't want her friend to get her hopes up only to have them dashed either. Which was why she knew what she needed to do.

JJ slipped down the hallway, holding her breath until she reached her room. Jonas always seemed to have a sixth sense about when she was up to something, so she could only hope to make it out of the penthouse without arousing any suspicion. But she couldn't just sit here wasting time if there was a chance she could find David and end this.

You don't even know exactly where he is.

JJ ignored the completely reasonable doubts rushing through her brain. It was true that she didn't know *exactly* where David was but if she knew the street, there was a good chance she could find him if she walked around. She knew *him*. She knew how his twisted mind worked. What he wanted was to break her down, scare her, and prove his dominance. That he could show up whenever he wanted and there was nothing she could do. It would be just like him to hang out a sign saying 'come find me JJ' just to fuck with her mind. As Matthias had pointed out, he clearly wasn't hiding.

Maybe if she gave him what he wanted, then he would give Isabella back and leave her friends out of this.

All she could do was pray that he hadn't hurt Isabella. Because if he had hurt her goddaughter, JJ was prepared to rain down whatever vengeance she could, even if she died trying.

Once she reached her room, she changed from her lounge clothes into jeans and a T-shirt. She avoided her own eyes in the mirror as she brushed out her hair and pulled it back into a high ponytail, the same way she'd worn it back when she'd been with David all those years ago. Her stomach clenched, disgusted at the idea of dressing to please him, but she reminded herself that this was for

Isabella. She could do anything, even flirt with a psycho, if it meant her best friend's daughter got to come home safe.

Her fingers hesitated over her favorite red lipstick. It wasn't the same color she'd worn as a teenager, but it was pretty damn close. Before she could overthink it, she swiped the crimson shade over her lips. Then she grabbed her handbag and walked out into the hallway.

No one was in the hallway, a small blessing, so she didn't waste any time going directly to the elevator and riding it down to the garage level. Her heart pounded furiously the entire time as she walked to her car, sure that at any moment Matthias would come running after her. The guy never seemed to sleep and had surveillance out the ass, so she could only pray that he was still distracted talking to Jonas. She didn't breathe normally until she pulled out of the garage and onto the street.

Then her heart started pounding for an entirely different reason. Every mile she covered was taking her closer to the source of all her nightmares. Her personal boogeyman. And she was placing herself right in his clutches.

JJ blanked her mind, clearing out all thoughts of how foolish this was, and focused on driving. When she saw an open meter she took it, even though she was still five blocks away. Walking would give her time to calm down and also the chance to scope out the neighborhood. She was familiar with the East Village, of course, as any long time resident of the city would be. It really wasn't the kind of place she'd expect David to settle. He'd always been obsessed with having and being the best. She wouldn't expect him to like the punk, modern vibe of this diverse neighborhood. The David she knew would have wanted to find the most expensive, exclusive place possible in the city.

A guy selling CDs tried to get her attention, and she shook her head with a smile. Any other day she'd probably have bought one just to help the kid out. But today she had a mission. When she finally reached 10th Street, her nerves were strung so tight she felt one deep breath away from snapping in two. Her eyes roamed both sides of the street, waiting. She wasn't sure exactly what she was looking for, only that she'd know it when she saw it.

Then her eyes landed on a shop across the street. The awning over the door had the store name in faded cursive.

Chameleon.

JJ stopped in her tracks, ignoring the muttered curses

from the people around her. That was it. It had to be. It was spelled differently than the code name he used but the coincidence was too much. Her hands tightened into fists. He thought he was really cute living above a store with his code name. This whole thing was one big joke to him.

She wasn't sure how long she stood there before she finally sprang into motion. Traffic was heavy, which made it even easier to dodge around the cars and taxis to get to the other side. Once there, she glared at the awning as if it could give her the answers she needed. Then as if she'd summoned him, he was there.

"David," she breathed.

To her surprise, he didn't seem alarmed that she was there. It was almost like he'd been expecting her.

"Jessica. There you are."

He smiled at her, as if she'd only gone out for coffee and he was welcoming her back home.

And JJ knew then that she'd made a terrible mistake.

fter talking over a few alternatives with Matthias, Jonas went straight for JJ's room and knocked. "JJ? You there?"

When she didn't answer, he opened the door and stuck his head in. Empty. All damn day he'd been dying to get to her. Sure, he'd only been gone three hours, but she'd been uncharacteristically quiet via text message. Normally by now she'd at least have butt-dialed him or something.

He backtracked and found Matthias still sitting in front of his laptop. "Hey, you seen my girlfriend?"

Matthias shook his head. "Nah, mate. But from the camera, I can see her purse isn't on the hook by the door.

Maybe she went out for some air. Maybe heading back to the office? She has a project she's working on. Do you want me to check her phone?"

A part of him wanted to tell the kid no, that he trusted JJ. He didn't want to confine her into a prison much like her old psycho ex had done. That's what he told himself. But the words were out of his mouth before he thought about them. "Yeah, would you?"

Matthias whirled his chair around. "Yeah, you got it." In seconds, Matthias frowned. "She's in the East Village. On 10th and —" suddenly Matthias dropped his head and kept shaking it. "For the love of Christ, is that woman mad?"

Jonas did not like the sound of that. "What do you mean?"

When Matthias looked at him, his eyes were bleak. "I don't want you to panic, but it looks like she's headed straight for West's place."

Ice doused Jonas's veins. "What the fuck? Who let her out of the house?"

Matthias put up his hands. "Easy mate. It's not like this is a prison. You and JJ both said you didn't want that for her. If that's what you wanted, I would've merrily locked her in her room, and she would've cussed me the fuck out. You know how she is. You know how she gets. You said you didn't want that. Which is fine by me, but we've all got to get on the same page. Either she's under protective custody, or she has freedom to move. But right now, how about we all just get down there and get her before she does something stupid."

Jonas shook his head. "No. I'm going. Do me a favor and alert Noah and the others. I might need backup."

Matthias nodded even as he jammed his ear comm unit in.

Jonas was out the door in a flash, just barely remembering to grab his keys for the SUV before running down to the garage. The elevator was too slow. He preferred the stairs, so at least he could physically *do* something.

The next ten minutes were an exercise in reckless driving. He navigated the streets like a complete maniac. Luckily, GPS and a proprietary software Matthias used directed him around all the traffic. And thankfully, he could park fucking anywhere. "Come on, come on, come on."

The last thing on earth he wanted to be was too late. Too late to stop her; too late to help her. When he saw her, he skidded the car to a stop right in front of a hydrant. Fuck, they could tow him if they liked. This was more important. In his ear, Matthias's voice rang clear. "Noah's on his way. Rafe too."

"Do me a favor and tell them to hurry."

As he approached, he saw that JJ was talking to someone. Right in front of the door of — oh fuck. Yeah, that was West, and JJ was reading him the fucking riot act.

To his credit, the guy was taking it and just insolently leaning against the doorframe. As JJ went all extra-JJ on him, her cursing was inventive. Her arms were gesticulating wildly. She was at desperation-level angry and Jonas picked up his pace, jogging to reach them. Before he could do anything, Chamaeleon pulled her close.

Mother Fucker. He held her so tight, JJ's arms and legs flailed. Jonas sprinted, his gun out of its holster and raised. "Let her go, asshole."

Over JJ's shoulder, the son of a bitch smirked. "As you wish. She came to me man. If you don't know how to keep your woman happy, don't put that on me." Then he shoved JJ away from him so hard that she fell on her ass. Then the bastard turned and went back inside.

What Jonas wanted to do was run in right after him. But

JJ was his main concern. She was shaking, and had curled herself into a little ball, rocking backward and forward. "Baby. Are you okay? Look at me. Tell me you're okay. I need to hear the words."

She nodded. "I'm — I'm okay. I—" She shook her head. "I'm so sorry. I know I shouldn't have come. But I couldn't sit around anymore and just wait. I overheard Matthias say he was here, and I thought if I just saw him and gave him what he wanted, he'd let Isabella go. But instead, he said he didn't know what I was talking about and called me crazy. And then I lost it. I know he's been watching me. I accused him and he said I was making it up and —"

The tears streamed down her face. Jonas bent down to his haunches and wrapped his arms around her. All he could do was hold her in the middle of the sidewalk with pedestrians streaming around them. He created a cocoon around her so that she was unaware of anyone else but him.

When Rafe and Noah showed up, he shook his head and inclined it toward the door. "He's in there."

Rafe patted himself down, doing an automatic weapons check. And then he headed straight for the door. But Noah clamped a hand on his shoulder. "No. I'm gonna tell you the same thing I told *him*." He inclined his head toward Jonas. "We can't go in weapons hot. He's a private citizen, and that's his residence. The FBI's handling that angle. Besides, we don't know what booby-traps he's got set up. And I don't want us barging in there and him hurting my fucking daughter."

Noah's voice wavered, and a jolt of pain sliced Jonas's heart in two. His woman and his best friend were in the most unimaginable pain, and there was nothing he could do about it. *What if you'd just taken a shot.* He could've just taken the guy out. And then they would have decreased their chances of finding Isabella.

In his arms, JJ started to shake. And all he could do was hold her tighter. He knew how terrified she was. He completely understood it. Because he was terrified, as well. The difference was he knew exactly what to do about it.

When he got his hands on David West, he was going to throw out all his opinions about due process and kill the fucker with his bare hands.

Jonas's hands shook as he clipped JJ into her seat. "Are you sure you're okay?"

She nodded. "Fine. I don't know what I was thinking. I just— if he hurts Isabella — I don't know what I'll do."

"We'll get her back." Jonas tucked her hair behind her ear. "But not by you going off half-cocked."

She smirked, and he knew that the old JJ was in there somewhere. "You said cock."

"And sooner or later I can show you mine. But first, let's get you home. Okay? Lucia's got enough on her mind without worrying that something is going to happen to you too."

She flushed and ducked her head. "I didn't mean to make anyone worry. I just — I just thought I could—"

"Thought you could trade yourself for the baby?"

JJ brought her head up and her eyes were grave. "She's a baby. She's never done anything to anyone. And all he wants is me. I can do that. I can do that for my friend. I can get her baby back."

Jonas took her shaking hands in his and dropped his forehead to hers. "Yeah, but at what cost? What would I do without you? What would *Lucia* do without you? Noah, Matthias, Oskar, Ryan, Dylan? All of us. You're family. And no one's sacrificing themselves. We fight. We don't give up. And you walking into that asshole's lair, volunteering yourself and not telling anyone where you're going... that's a *sacrifice*. We're not doing that. Besides, I will attest that you are no virgin. Not after what I've done to you." He winked. "Only fighters in our camp. Do you understand?"

She nodded but didn't answer.

Jonas slammed her door shut and tried to calm his temper while he walked around to the driver's side. Jesus Christ. Had he ever been so fucking scared in his life? That maniac could have taken her.

He could have killed her on the street, and they'd still be no closer to finding Isabella, and JJ would be gone. That woman was the most infuriating, stubborn, love of his life, and he'd almost lost her. *Shit.*

Before opening the driver's side door, he took a calming breath and then spoke into his comm unit. "All secure. She's in the car, we're heading back."

"You got it." Even Matthias sounded calmer. And he was almost always calm and efficient. Why couldn't JJ see how much they all cared about her? Why couldn't she understand that if she was lost, none of them would survive?

Jonas climbed under the wheel and patted her knee. "You ready to go home?"

She nodded, but her eyes were still distant. He understood. It was that feeling of being completely impotent; of knowing that you needed to do *something*, but having no idea what to do. Yeah, he knew that feeling all too well.

Jonas wove effortlessly into the traffic downtown, ready to make a turn and head back up to the penthouse when Matthias's voice was crisp and clipped in his ear. "All hands. All hands. Chamaeleon spotted leaving his apartment. He's wearing a baby carrier and what looks like a baby. Headed east on 14th Street. All hands, I repeat all hands."

Jonas tapped his comm. "Roger. Turning around."

Noah's voice came over the comm unit clearly. "Rafe and I are closer."

Next to Jonas, JJ stiffened. "What's happening?"

Jonas whipped the car around in an illegal U-turn and

headed back in the direction they'd come. "Chamaeleon left his place. Wearing a baby carrier."

Her mouth dropped open. "I *knew* it."

Jonas had nothing to say. She had known it. She'd gone there to get the baby back and he'd stopped her.

No. You stopped her from getting herself killed. There was no way to know he had Isabella for sure.

"I know. We're going to get her back." The words sounded empty to his ears. But what else was he supposed to say? How else was he supposed to soothe her? Traffic came to a complete standstill, and he cursed before whipping his car into oncoming traffic, swerving to avoid collision with the cars and taxis that blared their horns at him.

When he whipped back into his appropriate lane, he'd cut out at least 10 car-lengths of traffic. When he arrived back on 16th Street, Noah whizzed by him and he followed, giving chase. "Matthias, where is he now?"

"He's turning left on Liberty Street. Zuccotti Park. No cars. Only pedestrians, you're gonna have to get out and run."

Jonas slid a glance at JJ. "What are the chances if I parked the car and asked you to sit here, that you'll listen?"

"Probably about as high as you letting me cut off your dick and carry it around in my purse."

"Fair enough. In that case, keep up. Be aware. Don't let him catch you."

"What's happening?" She already had her seatbelt off.

"He's turned left up above."

In his ear comm he could hear Noah panting. "Giving chase. Rafe is headed around to cut him off."

Jonas pulled right up to another fire hydrant, not giving any fucks that he'd parked illegally, and he was out of car in a flash. JJ yelled, "Right behind you." He was desperate to get to Noah and find Isabella. But he was also desperate to keep JJ safe. He knew how these guys thought. Well, at least he'd been told snippets by Noah. This could all be a trap. And he wasn't letting JJ out of his sight. Eventually he just gave up and took her hand and dragged her behind him.

To her credit, she followed quickly, didn't ask too many questions, and ran like there was some kind of sample sale.

They cut up to Noah who was spinning around in circles. "Matthias? Where the fuck did he go?"

"He cut across the grass. To your right. Blue baseball hat."

They saw him and sure enough, he was wearing a baseball cap and the damn baby carrier.

Noah had his gun out of the holster in a second, and Jonas had to remind him, "Noah, I know, but fucking civilians."

"You don't think I have a head shot?"

"I think you do, but things happen all the time. And this could be some kind of trap. So put the gun away, and run your ass off."

JJ was panting so hard Jonas was afraid she might fall. But she kept up, and the two of them ran. Then up ahead, Chamaeleon stopped. He turned right before the pond in the park and then took the baby out of the carrier. When they were within thirty feet of him, he held the baby over the Koi pond.

Noah screamed. "Don't. She's a baby. She's done nothing to you."

The fucker smirked. "I don't give a fuck. It's not her I care about. It's *her*." His gaze locked on JJ. And next to him Jonas could feel her stiffen.

JJ ran forward. "You can have me." Jonas tried to grasp her

hand, but her palm was sweaty and slipped right out of his. "I'll come with you. Just put Isabella down. I'll come with you. Whatever you want. Just leave the baby alone."

"No. Not like this. Not while your friends have shooters aimed at me. You'll come with me eventually. You and I *are* going to be together, but I'd rather us have our conversation without an audience. So you can come after me, or you can save the baby." And then he tossed Isabella into the pond.

"No!" JJ screamed as she Jonas and Noah all ran straight for the baby.

Jonas knew they were making the wrong choice. One of them needed to go after Chamaeleon. He tapped his comm. "Rafe. He's headed West. Through the park. You go after him. We have Isabella."

Noah was in the pond faster than any of them, lifting his legs and wading through the water until he reached the baby. Then he screamed so loud and so low that Jonas was pretty sure the earth shook.

"Noah. Noah, is she alive?"

His friend lifted his head, the anguish drawing all his

features down. "No." He shook his head. "It's not even her. It's another doll. But this one is fucking animated."

Jonas cursed under his breath "Son of a bitch."

JJ dropped to her knees inside the pond, the water coming up to her waist. "This is on me. He wants me. And I don't know how to help."

CHAPTER FOUR

Jonas had never felt more helpless in his life.

Watching JJ break down, falling to her knees right in the middle of the pond, took him to a dark place. One he wasn't sure he could crawl back from. He'd been down this road before, watching a woman he loved being terrorized and broken down, piece by piece.

But fuck that. He'd be damned if he'd just watch as JJ slowly lost everything that made up her ballsy, flat-out, fearless self. Maybe that was what gave him the idea to approach Noah with the most insane idea ever.

Once the team had returned to the penthouse, Jonas

pulled Rafe and Noah aside and floated his idea. He was met with are-you-fucking-kidding-me glares.

"You want us to go to the head of ORUS and ask for his help apprehending one of his own agents?" Noah shook his head, like he wasn't sure he'd heard correctly.

"I know it sounds crazy," Jonas muttered.

Noah glared at him. "It doesn't just sound crazy. It is crazy. Normally I'd approach Ian with an offer, maybe some information he needed in exchange for a favor. But this is one of his guys; an active ORUS agent."

Everything his friend was saying made sense. Hell it made perfect sense not to walk right into the fucking lion's den and announce your presence, but Jonas was done sitting around and waiting for that fucker West to make a move. So far David had been the one calling the shots, arranging them all where he wanted them like chess pieces on a board. They needed to turn things around, pull him out of hiding on *their* terms.

Noah made a frustrated sound. "Even if he believes us when we have no proof, there's no guarantee that he'd help us. Ian is better than most, that's why we installed him as the head of ORUS. Better the enemy you know, right? But I'm not sure I trust him that much. We could be walking right into a trap. For all we know, this is exactly what Chamaeleon wants us to do."

"I don't think so," Jonas said softly. His mind flashed back to the way West had looked at JJ. It hadn't been calculated at all. He'd been wearing an expression of utter obsession, one that made Jonas's skin crawl even as he remembered it.

"You didn't see the way he was looking at her. He wants JJ, and he's willing to do whatever is necessary to get to her. I seriously doubt Ian wants a loose cannon like that out there possibly putting ORUS at risk. He might not want to help us, but if he can rein West in, he might help us inadvertently."

Noah stood, his face a blank mask. He left the room and returned a couple of minutes later with Matthias and Oskar.

"This is the deal. Jonas thinks we should get Ian involved."

Matthias opened his mouth to protest but Noah held up a hand.

"Believe me, I know. But he has some good points. Ian might be the only one who can actually control West, and we think that might give us the opening we need to figure out where he's keeping Isabella."

No one spoke for a few moments, and Jonas knew they were all thinking the same thing. It might help them, or it might piss David off. And if that were the case, who knew how he'd react?

Matthias acted as a voice of reason. "Maybe we shouldn't—"

"This is the only thing we can do," Noah cut him off. "The longer he has her, the less likely it is that she'll still be alive when we find her. This has to work."

Rafe's voice was calm but deadly. "You know me. I'm behind you all the way."

For the next hour, they discussed strategy and then armed themselves to the teeth from the armory room. Ryan and Dylan were going to stay behind to protect the women, something Jonas was sure he'd get an earful about later. JJ hated it when they went off leaving the "little women" behind but Jonas wasn't sure how she wanted them to handle it. He didn't want to shut her out, but he for damn sure wasn't going to bring her into a dangerous situation.

He'd noticed Noah had been taking more time to reassure

Lucia lately, telling her what he was doing before leaving, which was unlike him. Jonas smiled thinking of how stoic and unbending his friend had been before finally admitting his longtime feelings for Lucia.

They took three separate vehicles with Rafe on his own, Matthias and Oskar in one of the vans they used for surveillance, and Jonas and Noah in the SUV. When they left New York, Jonas glanced over at Noah.

"He's meeting us at the X." The X was the location that ORUS used for mission prep. They never ever discussed details of black ops in their shiny office uptown. The X's location changed monthly.

Jonas shrugged. It was an odd meeting place but he knew better than to ask too many questions. It had been years before Noah had confided in him about his past with the borderline-legal, government-sanctioned, shadow organization known as ORUS. He'd figured out on his own that Matthias had been in, too, and with the things Noah had mentioned about Rafe, he was pretty sure Lucia's older brother was also a former agent. It made sense given the timeline of when Noah said he'd come into the DeMarco's lives. Plus, the way Rafe fought indicated he was either an ORUS agent or former special ops. The dude had beaten the hell out of Matthias and Oskar and had almost blinded Jonas. He rubbed his eyes absently at the memory.

Not that he was still bitter or anything.

When they pulled up outside of the X, Noah parked and got out immediately. Jonas followed, his eyes scanning the surroundings. Rafe appeared silently at his side. Matthias and Oskar climbed out of the van.

"There's no one stationed to the East or the South."

Jonas nodded once just as Rafe appeared.

"Looks clear. Let's get this shit over with." Rafe's hand hovered close to the piece in his waistband.

They climbed over the metal guardrail and made their way down closer to the water. Ian stood next to a trashcan where a fire burned. Anyone looking would see nothing more than a random bum warming himself by a fire.

Not the head of a secretive and lethal organization. Maybe that was part of the lesson they all had to learn, Jonas thought. Not to judge too easily because nothing was truly as it appeared.

Noah stood next to Ian, stretching his hands out to the heat of the fire. Ian didn't acknowledge him in any way.

"One of your dogs is off his leash," Noah finally said.

Ian grunted. "My dogs don't have leashes, they have microchips. If there's a problem, I'll take care of it. Not sure why that warrants a trip to this shithole so I can freeze my ass off."

"It warrants a hell of a lot when my daughter's life is at stake. You brought a predator into my home, and now I need you to help take him down."

Ian froze and then turned slowly to look at Noah. "Chamaeleon?" The word was barely a whisper, but Noah nodded curtly. "Why would you think it was him? He's been overseas for years and just got back. If he was after you, why would he wait this long?"

"It's not me he's after. It's a friend. Isabella just got caught in the crossfire."

Ian glanced behind him at Jonas and the others then barked out a laugh. "Well, you certainly came with a show of force."

"This is my daughter, Ian. I need your help. I made you Orion because I thought you'd be different."

Ian scoffed. "Like that was some favor. Might as well have painted a permanent target on my back."

"Don't fuck with me, Ian!"

Noah's outburst took them all by surprise, Oskar shifting restlessly while Matthias clenched his fists. Jonas wanted to put a hand on Noah's shoulder but under the circumstances, his friend was likely to bite it off. The only one who didn't move was Rafe. He just stood staring at Ian with the blank visage of a man who had no trouble killing to get what he wanted.

Jonas shook his head. It was Rafe's niece at stake, after all. The dude was a stone cold killer, but the only people he ever looked at with love were the grandmother who'd raised him, Lucia, and the mischievous baby girl who'd brought them all so much joy.

Chamaeleon had no idea what he'd started. Things had escalated from a skirmish to a full-scale nuclear war the moment he'd taken Isabella.

Ian finally spoke when it seemed they'd settled a bit.

"I'll handle this. He's still in contact so I can have someone bring him in. Alive."

Noah let out an anguished sound that hit Jonas right in the chest. It was the sound of a man who was close to losing it. They needed to get out of there before he did something to make Ian take back his tentative offer to help.

"Let's go. Maybe one of the boys has something by now."

Noah nodded silently but his pain hung in the air between them, so thick it was choking them all. They turned to leave but before they got more than a few feet, Ian's voice floated from behind them.

"I'll handle him this time, Leo. But if you ever come at me like this again, be prepared for your funeral."

Noah turned and nailed the other man with a dark stare. In that moment, Jonas realized he was seeing the true Noah, the killer ORUS had trained him to be underneath the civilized mask he wore everyday.

"If anything happens to my daughter, we'll all be dead. Because that's the only way I'm not getting her back."

———

JJ rolled over and buried her face in the pillowcase. Even after a hot shower and wrapping herself in one of Jonas's shirts and a huge robe, she still couldn't seem to get warm. This was a different type of cold, the kind that got into your bones and made you feel like you were being punished.

Maybe I am.

JJ pulled the covers up to her chin and tried to sleep, only because she'd promised Jonas that she would. A tear slipped over the bridge of her nose to dampen the pillow. She bit her lip to make sure she wasn't making any noise. The last thing she wanted was to raise Lucia's suspicions even more.

Noah had asked them not to tell Lucia what had happened. They'd only told her that JJ had gone to confront him and that he'd pushed her. Although she was pretty sure Lucia wasn't buying their story anyway. Even though she didn't agree with Noah's decision to keep Lucia in the dark, a small, secret part of her was thankful. She wasn't sure she could bear to look her best friend in the eye and admit that she didn't think David was going to give Isabella back.

She shivered remembering the satisfied look in his eyes when he'd seen her standing outside. He was getting off on this, on the power to draw her to him against her will. It was terrifying and humiliating, but she'd have gladly borne all of that if it brought Izzy back.

There was a quick knock on the door before Lucia stuck her head in. JJ sat up, wiping her tears on the sleeve of her robe.

"Hey, you can come in. I'm not sleeping anyway."

Lucia shut the door behind her. JJ moved over so Lucia could sit on the edge of the bed.

"I wanted to check on you and see if you were really okay, not just pretending so Jonas wouldn't worry." Lucia's gray eyes roamed over her as if looking for bruises.

It only made JJ's stomach churn harder. Her friend was so loving and nurturing, they'd always joked that Lucia would have all the babies and JJ could just be the crazy aunt who sneaked them candy and told them inappropriate stories about men once they were older.

What would happen to her friend if they couldn't rescue Isabella? It would destroy her. It was the worst thing in the world to see destruction coming for you on the horizon when you were locked in place and could do nothing to stop it.

"I'm okay. Physically."

Lucia pushed her hair back. "That's not what I asked."

JJ sucked in a tremulous breath. "He's insane, Lucia. I don't know what to do. He was enjoying it, denying everything and watching me lose it. I don't know what he'll do next, but I am terrified. I bet Noah is wishing you'd never met me."

"We can't give up. I have to believe that there's a purpose to all of this." Lucia lay down next to her and grabbed her hand. "And Noah loves you like a sister, just like I do. Everyone here loves you. I'll have to keep telling you that until you finally believe it."

"If you don't mind, Lucia, I'll take over from here."

Jonas's deep voice cut through the room, startling them both. Lucia squeezed her hand before getting up. She patted Jonas on the arm on the way out.

"Hey," JJ said finally, not sure what else to say. Part of her was afraid to ask exactly where he'd been. She wasn't sure she could take any more bad news today.

"Hey," Jonas whispered back before lying down next to her. He rolled over so their lips were only a few inches apart. "You should listen to your friend, you know. Everyone here loves you. You're not just someone they put up with to make Lucia happy. They adore you in your own right."

JJ closed her eyes, mortified that he could zero in on her insecurities so easily. It was impossible to hold any resentment toward Lucia, even though she was the delicately beautiful, feminine ideal that JJ had never quite been able to meet. Lucia was all sweetness and light while JJ was all gunpowder and hot sauce. She couldn't help that there were definitely times when she'd felt people only tolerated her because she was friends with Lucia.

"I love them, too. That's why this is so hard. Being here is putting them all at risk. It's selfish of me to stay. I should just run away, somewhere David will never find me."

Jonas grabbed her so suddenly she squeaked. In the next few seconds, she found herself pressed beneath two hundred pounds of pissed-off but completely aroused male. He flexed his hips, driving his hard cock between her legs. JJ moaned at the contact, the pressure hitting right where she ached.

"First of all, you aren't going *anywhere.*" He kissed her on the neck, sucking right over her pulse. "Second of all, if you run, I'll follow you. There's nothing I wouldn't do for you, Jessica Jones."

One minute she was staring into his eyes, the next she was wrapped around him, her legs twined with his and her arms clamped around his neck. He was what she needed, that port in the storm that made her feel safe.

JJ held on to him for dear life, kissing every bit of skin within reach. Maybe she could merge into him and lose this desperate feeling of isolation. Jonas seemed to understand what she wanted because he kissed her for long moments, tangling their tongues together while holding her closer, one of his big hands tucked under her ass, holding her in place for the slow, rolling movement of his hips.

"I've got you, baby," he whispered.

JJ moaned when he bit her lip gently. She clutched at him, trying to get his shirt off. Jonas chuckled as he moved back slightly so she could tug at the cotton. "Take it easy, baby. I'm not going anywhere."

But JJ didn't want to take it easy. She wanted it fast and hard, wanted to feel him everywhere. Anything to cover the feeling David's eyes had painted on her skin.

"Faster, Jonas. Please."

He raised his head, and whatever he saw in her eyes made him move. One arm reached behind him, and he yanked the shirt off in one smooth motion. JJ was on him immediately running her hands greedily over the golden brown skin revealed. He moaned low in his throat when she slid down and sucked at his nipples.

"Christ, you're trying to kill me."

JJ was lost in the sight, sensation and feel of his skin against her mouth. He tasted slightly salty and uniquely masculine. She tugged and yanked until she tossed the robe aside. Suddenly he flipped her over, his weight covering her back, pressing her into the mattress.

"Hold on, angel. I know what you need."

He grabbed her hands and pushed them over her head. She struggled slightly at first, but a gentle kiss to her cheek made her relax. Just like that, she melted, completely safe in his embrace. He was going to take her, comfort her, pleasure her, and all she had to do was trust it.

Trust him.

"I need you, Jonas." The admission felt like swallowing rocks. JJ wondered if she'd ever felt safe enough to admit that she needed anyone before.

"I know you do, baby girl. I'm going to take care of you."

She reared up off the bed when his fingers made contact with the edge of her panties. Every touch, every brush of his lips against hers felt like live wires. Her skin was starving for him and so was she.

"Jesus, you're soaked for me already." His voice was husky with desire and purely masculine appreciation.

JJ normally would have made a smart comment, but her breath was stolen at the first thrust of his fingers. She cried out, remembering at the last minute that the others might be able to hear them and biting her lip.

His mouth covered hers, sucking gently at the lip she'd abused. JJ let out a greedy sound as she ran her hands over his muscles. All the guys were in great shape, it was a prerequisite for their line of work, but none of them could compare to Jonas in her opinion. He was built on the slimmer side but his workout regime had packed his frame with muscle. She loved the feeling of him pressing into her.

He tugged at the edge of her shirt and she held her arms over her head so he could pull it off. Jonas groaned at the sight of her in nothing but her panties. JJ lifted her hips so she could pull the panties down her legs, her eyes taking in his every motion as he struggled to get out of his boots and jeans. He hadn't worn any underwear so as soon as he tugged his jeans down, his cock bobbed out, thick and ready. JJ leaned forward and sucked on the tip.

"Christ. JJ, you can't do that. I won't last, baby" he warned.

She smiled around him, reveling in his erotic curse as she hummed against his skin. His fingers tangled in her hair and she moaned again, incredibly turned on by the sharp tug at her roots. When she looked up at him, Jonas was watching her with slitted eyes, taking in the sight of her lips wrapped around his swollen cock.

Something in her eyes must have set him off, because he tugged her back gently and then pushed her back on the bed. JJ started to protest but then lost her train of thought at the first touch of his skin against hers. His skin was so warm, burning against hers and she wanted to feel it all over her. But Jonas had other ideas, nuzzling her breast before sucking her tight nipple between his lips. He alternated between her breasts until JJ thought she'd scream, and then she did cry out when he entered her a moment later, his thick cock stretching her to the limit.

"Oh my god." JJ bit him on the shoulder, and his hiss of surprise mingled with her harsh breathing. It was all she could do to hang on, clutching his shoulders as he rolled his hips. As he tunneled deeper, she felt like they were melting into each other. That was what JJ wanted, to be overtaken and overpowered. To know that Jonas was in control and wouldn't let anything bad happen.

She needed to believe that.

"I'm not going to let anything happen to you, baby. Believe that. You mean too much to me." Jonas pushed the hair off her face and the motion was so tender it brought tears to her eyes. "I love you, JJ."

"I love you, too. So much."

JJ shuddered as waves of pleasure spread through her like lightning bolts. It was a struggle to keep her eyes open, but she didn't want to miss a thing. Jonas didn't disappoint her either, his face tightening a few moments later as he fought his own release.

"Come with me, baby."

As soon as he said the words, JJ let go, flying into a storm of light and sensation. His hands tightened under her bottom, and she heard his sexy-as-hell growl as he let go. The last thing she heard before she drifted off was Jonas telling her to rest and that she was safe with him.

CHAPTER FIVE

J onas's fucking eyes hurt. The throbbing had started behind his orbital bone as soon as they'd come back from the damn park yesterday. The motherfucker had played them. *All of them.*

West had known he was under surveillance the whole time. He knew exactly where the cameras were, he knew exactly what moves they would make. Because they were moves that *he* would make. Because West and Noah had been trained by the same people. And so Blake Security had come up against a dead-end.

Jonas still couldn't imagine the kind of pain that Noah was going through—to think that he had his child and then to have that hope ripped away from him, knowing the man who had done it had gotten away with it.

Jonas had begged his friend to take some time off, but Noah wasn't having it. He said other people needed them too. But really, he could see Noah fraying at the edges. Lucia was practically catatonic. Matthias was still blaming himself. And JJ, well JJ was basically a shell of herself. He had no idea how to help except to be there.

So he'd camped out at the penthouse, but he needed fresh clothes and a fucking moment to think. Because right now his best friend wasn't thinking clearly, and the woman he loved was blaming herself for everything. He needed a little separation to figure out what the fuck to do and then he'd go right back. Right back into the fray and support the people he loved most the best way he knew how.

He parked his car in the garage and took the private elevator up, the tension rolling in his shoulders. Jesus, all he needed was a shower, and a good night's sleep. The problem was sleep was hard to come by at the moment. Because every time anyone closed their eyes, all they thought about was Isabella and if she was okay. The good news was the nanny had seemed anti-murder, so very likely the baby was still alive.

Yeah, because that's a small favor.

He would still thank God for it, because after that bullshit meeting with Ian, they didn't have much else.

When the elevator doors opened, the hairs on the back of his neck stood at attention. Something was wrong.

He had his gun out of his holster and in his palm without even blinking. The closer he got to the apartment, the more his body gave him that heebie-geebie, creepy-crawly feeling. Something was definitely off. He walked to his apartment cautiously, and studied the door for any hints of a break in. But there weren't any. Not even scratches on the doorknob to indicate someone had attempted to pick it.

Cautiously he stood to the side and tried to turn the knob. It gave way easily. *Oh fuck.* The door was unlocked. And he'd most definitely locked it after the last time he was here.

Plus, his alarm system didn't go off. The moment that door opened, his phone should've chimed. But it didn't. Someone had disarmed it.

For the love of fuck.

Cautiously he stepped in, and cleared the main foyer and then the kitchen.

Even though the hairs on his arms were now standing at attention, he had a feeling that the apartment was empty. And then he walked into the living room.

No. No. No. No. No. No.

Blood. Everywhere. "Oh Jesus. Jesus Christ." His hand slapped for the lights on the wall. In the middle of his living room Katie was sprawled in a pool of her own blood. Oh God. And there was a baby carrier turned away from him.

His heart hammered, and his mouth went dry. *Oh God. No. Not Isabella. Please. God no.*

He ran over to the carrier and found Isabella seated in the center. Her mouth was partially open, tongue out, and she was sucking merrily on it as if it was a nipple. Oh thank fuck, she was asleep. *She's alive.*

His phone was out in a second, dialing number one on the speed dial. Noah answered before it even finished ringing "What's wrong?"

"Katie's dead. She's at my apartment. Isabella's alive. I have her."

"Motherfucker. Are you sure the apartment's empty?"

Fuck. He'd been so worried about Isabella he hadn't finished clearing. He quickly turned on his security feed then manually cleared the two bedrooms, the bathroom, the pantry, and the closets.

"No one's here. Isabella's asleep. The nanny is dead, Noah. There is blood —" And then he heard the sirens and saw the flashing lights outside. "Noah. The police are already here."

"Don't say anything. I'll have the lawyer at the station to bail you out before you even get there."

"Noah, he was here. He did this on purpose. I'm not leaving the baby here on her own. Otherwise I'd –"

"Thank you, Jonas. Oskar and I are on our way."

Jonas had no choice, he wasn't leaving Isabella here. Not without her parents, not without someone who would at least look after her until they could get here.

The police came right to his apartment with guns raised. As if they knew exactly where he would be and what they would find.

He set Isabella down gently and raised his hands. "I'm on the job. I work for Blake Security."

One of the officers that had barged in first had to turn quickly and take a deep breath at the sight of the room. *Yeah, welcome to the shit show.* There was a lot of blood. The other officers yelled at him to get his hands in the air and he complied.

"Like I said, my identification is in my right breast pocket. I work for Blake Security. We're a security firm. I have a license for concealed carry. I came in and found her like this along with the baby. The baby's fine. Her parents are Noah and Lucia Blake. They've been notified of where to find her."

"You didn't call an ambulance first?"

"I knew right away she was dead. You know the pool of blood is kind of a major indicator."

"Oh, you're a smart ass then?" The officer wrenched his arm behind his back, and Jonas cursed.

"No, I'm not being a smart ass. I'm just giving you the necessary information so you can do your job."

"We'll tell you what we need from you. You have the right to remain silent."

Jonas was going to exercise that right. At least now Lucia

and Noah had their daughter back safe. That was all that mattered.

As they perp-walked him out of the building, some of his neighbors scuttled back into their apartments, shocked and frowning. Right now he didn't give a shit what happened to him. He knew to keep his mouth shut, but as they tugged him out to the car through the small crowd forming with their ubiquitous cell phones trained on him, he saw the man he was looking for across the street.

For a second he forgot himself and struggled against the cuffs. But the cops were on him with swiftness and shoved him back in the car. All Jonas could do was stare at David West as he was driven away.

He didn't know how, and he didn't know when, but he was going to kill that fucker.

———

JJ had been so trained to look for Jonas when she exited her office, she didn't even notice right away that it wasn't him who was driving until she yanked open the door. "Hey, any news? Oh —"

Oskar gave her a wry smile. "Sorry, it's just my pretty face. No ridiculously expensive threads today."

"Oh is Jonas busy today? Has there been any news on Isabella?"

Oskar's handsome face morphed into a tight-lipped frown. "Yeah, there's been a development."

"Tell me." JJ climbed into the passenger seat and clicked on her seatbelt. "Do we know where David is? Do we have a sighting on Isabella?"

"We don't just have a sighting on Isabella, we have her. She's at the hospital right now with Noah and Lucia, getting checked out."

"Oh my God." She doubled over in the seat, clutching her hands on her knees, as a wave of nausea rolled through her. "Did that bastard hurt her?"

He shook his head. "Didn't look like it. She'd been fed and taken care of. We think he gave her something to sedate her, but other than that she's probably going to be okay."

"Oh my God. I've been so worried. Where did they find her? Where did he leave her? Did he —"

Oskar shook his head. "I don't have any other answers. All

I know is that *we* have her, and it looks like she's gonna be okay."

JJ nodded, the relief chasing away some of the nausea, but the spike of adrenaline made her hands shake. "Okay. Thank God. So what now, did we kill David?"

He shook his head. "Fucker wasn't there."

JJ slid him a glance. "Oskar, if you want to keep your balls intact, I suggest you start telling me everything from the beginning. If we have Isabella back, why do you look even more German and stoic than before? And where the hell is Jonas?"

His lips thinned again. "JJ. I'm sorry. When Jonas went home this afternoon, he walked in to find Katie dead in his living room in a pool of blood. A lot of it. Matthias tapped into Jonas's security feed to get a good look at what the cops were seeing. Isabella was there in her carrier, apparently mostly unharmed. But the police arrested Jonas."

JJ stared at him. "And you couldn't fucking lead with that? They arrested him? Take me to the police station right now. I swear to God I'm going to rip someone a new one. He works for a security company, for the love of Christ —"

Oskar held up his hand. "Look, I know. I know this is upsetting. I was instructed to take you back to the penthouse."

She raised a brow. "The hell you will. You're gonna take those brawny shoulders of yours and you're going to drive me straight to the police station because I am going to get him out. If you don't, your nuts will be your dinner tonight."

"Jesus, woman. No need to threaten my balls. Listen, we have the lawyer on it okay? He's going to get a bail hearing. Normally, it wouldn't happen until tomorrow, but he's making it happen tonight. The lawyer's on it. There's not much you can do."

"I swear before God, I will fill your bed full of dildos that vibrate if you do not get me to Jonas this instant."

Oskar's eyes widened. "Seriously, woman, what is wrong with you? How do you even come up with shit that diabolical?"

"Don't be such a prude Oskar, you might like a dildo."

The German surprised her when he gave her a wolfish grin. It completely transformed his face, making him seem carefree and roguish and showing off the full brightness of his handsome features. Jesus Christ, it was a good thing the guy barely smiled.

"Oh, I know what to do with a dildo and a woman. It can help enhance the experience in so many ways. But a bed full of them? You're just being cruel now. My bed's empty, so what am I going to do with a dildo?"

JJ grinned. "Well, I have a few ideas. They involve shoving them where the —"

Oskar shook his head. "You know what, keep that to yourself. My instructions are to take you home, so that's where we're going."

"And I swear to God if you do not take me to Jonas right now, I will cut off your balls in your sleep."

"You think I'm gonna let you close to my balls?"

She sat back and crossed her arms, smiling beatifically. "Well, you do like those cookies I make. All I have to do is drug one of them, and then you'll pretty much let anyone do anything."

His mouth fell open, and he stared at her. "Jesus. Fine. There's no need to get nasty. I'll take you to him. But let me call it in to Matthias first. Then maybe he can send Dylan to meet us so that at least you'll be protected. Don't forget, West is still out there, and he wants you. Jonas won't forgive any of us if anything happens to you."

"Well, Jonas is just going to have to deal. Because this time, I'm going to be there for him."

"I swear to God. You women might be more trouble than you're worth."

"Said every man ever, but still all you boys keep coming to the yard don't you?"

"Ain't that the truth?"

CHAPTER SIX

J onas didn't exactly know how to walk with his JJ blanket. The moment he'd been released on bond, JJ had attached herself to his side and refused to let him go.

Not that he was angry about that at all. All he wanted to do was hold onto her tight. Right about now he might never let go of her. His lawyer had already notified him that Isabella was fine and that she was just at the hospital getting checked out. So at least that weight was off his mind.

And JJ was with him. So as far as he was concerned, all was right with the world. The only thing left hanging was the question of how many ways they could kill David West.

The moment the elevator doors to the penthouse opened, Jonas was enveloped by a simultaneous feeling of security and chaos. The whole crew was in attendance. Dylan, Ryan, Matthias, Oskar. Rafe was on a job, but he'd be in later.

Even the team doctor was there. Noah had probably called him just in case Jonas needed anything for shock. Which was ridiculous because he was fine. Though, he couldn't deny he'd been more than a little alarmed at the possibility of spending the night in jail. The thought of running into anyone he'd helped put away years ago made him a little twitchy.

Everyone gave him the awkward man hugs, and then from the back room he heard a baby cry. His heart stuttered for a moment.

Lucia came out from around the back hallway, with Isabella in her arms. "Someone heard her Godfather was home, so she insisted on seeing you."

Jonas's gaze went straight to hers. "Is she okay?"

Lucia nodded and nuzzled her daughter's cheek. "Yeah. She's perfectly fine. It seems like she wants to be held by her godfather."

JJ released him, and he missed her warmth immediately. But when Lucia placed a squirming Isabella in his arms, he had to fight back the stinging in his eyes. "Hello, Angel. We had quite a fright looking for you. I'm so glad you're okay."

Isabella reached up with a tiny fist, and Jonas was pretty sure he was about to get hit in the nose again. But then she opened her little hand and patted him gently on the cheek as if to say, *It's okay. I'm fine. You worry too much.* And then she made a series of very loud baby sounds. As if she was really trying to have a conversation with him.

Unfortunately, he didn't speak a word of baby, so he held her and rocked her instead, whispering little cooing sounds. After a moment she scrunched her face and kicked her little feet before letting out a wail.

Lucia giggled. "She's hungry. I think they were feeding her formula at the hospital. She probably didn't like it, so I need to go and feed her real quick if that's okay."

Jonas nodded. "Of course." He gave the baby back to Lucia and lifted his gaze to find Noah leaning against the wall.

"You good, Noah?"

His friend wiped at his eyes with the back of his hand. "Yeah. I'm good. She's home. So, I'm trying to be grateful for that and calm my murdering instinct."

"I have the same instinct," Jonas said.

JJ tugged on his hand. "Can we not talk about murder for just a minute? Okay? We just got him home."

Everyone followed them into the living room, the men taking their usual spots; which meant Oskar and Matthias on opposing sides of the main couch, fighting over the remote control; Ryan, as usual, by the door looking for his fastest possible exit; and Dylan, as he was the youngest and wanting to prove himself the most, taking his ever-watchful post at the window. Even though he knew no one could get up here. *Not anymore, anyway.*

Anyone who wanted to try would have to bypass biometrics and a series of security checkpoints below. It was no cakewalk getting up into this penthouse now. But still, he watched the street.

JJ liked the softer couch by the window so she sat in it, and Jonas followed easily, wrapping his arm around her. God he loved this woman. He was so happy to be home. Noah just leaned against the wall and watched them all.

"So, when Rafe gets back from watch, we need to figure out a plan."

Matthias nodded from the couch. "I vote to kill him. Fuck Orion, mate. He's known this whole time where that wanker was and who he is. He's known that West was stalking JJ. He needs to be put down like a rabid dog."

Jonas nodded. "I wanted to kill him days ago. But *you* guys stopped me."

Matthias shook his head. "Rafe and I were down for it. Look at *him*," he inclined his head at Noah. "He was the one who said we couldn't kill him."

Noah nodded. "I know what I said. And I stand by my decision then. Because that was the information we had at the time. But now we have new information, so I'm all down for the plan of killing the asshole."

JJ raised a hand. "You guys know I'm still here right? And you're just casually talking about killing people?"

Matthias flushed a little, but he asked, "You don't want us to kill him?"

Beside Jonas, JJ stiffened. "No. Are you insane?"

He could only stare at her. "You don't want us to kill him?"

She shook her head. "No. Of course not." She turned to face him. "I want to do it myself. I want to get close enough to him to stab him in the nuts and keep stabbing him until he dies."

A thick silence fell over the room with every single one of the guys wincing.

Jonas shuddered. "Wow, okay. A for enthusiasm. But we're not letting you anywhere near him. He's dangerous."

"So am I. He tried to hurt me. And then he took my best friend's baby. And then he sent my man to jail. So pardon me if I want a little bit of payback."

Jonas shook his head and only held her closer. Jesus he loved her. "You really do know how to pick them sweetheart. Your ex is one sick fuck. Good thing I am too."

"So you'll let me kill him?"

From the wall, Noah vetoed this. "No. No reason you should have all the fun, JJ. We're going to come up with a plan that we can all agree to. And then Chamaeleon is going to stop breathing. Posthaste."

———

The bottom had fallen out of JJ's world. David had planned a fresh kind of hell for all of them, and they'd all fallen right into his trap.

She had to fight the rage she felt every time she thought about how he'd managed to put a man like Jonas in jail. They were lucky they'd gotten him out so quickly.

Oh, her man was strong. And he was tough. And to hang with this gang, he was clearly a fighter. Maybe he was even capable of being a killer. But he was just, and he wouldn't go looking for a fight. He wouldn't put someone down just to prove that he was the biggest, baddest guy on the block or whatever the hell they called it in prison. And if he was unwilling to kill for his own survival, that refusal would get him killed in prison. Especially once everyone found out he was a former cop.

Even though she'd known the team had it covered, she'd been scared. For those forty-five minutes she'd been at the police station waiting for him to be released, she'd been terrified.

The lawyer on retainer had been waiting at the station before Jonas had even been brought in. And he had the time-stamped footage of Jonas leaving Blake security, proving that Jonas couldn't have killed that girl.

They'd been out in forty-five minutes. And just in case that hadn't done the trick, Matthias had been on standby to hack whatever system the police used and pretty much make Jonas disappear from existence. Matthias had a new name and new identity ready to go for him if it had come to that. But that would have meant Jonas would have to disappear for a while.

Which was fine by her, as long as Matthias made her one, too. Because there was no way Jonas was going anywhere without her. *Fact.*

But it hadn't come to that. The police didn't have enough to hold him, but since Katie had died in his apartment, he was still a person of interest. But JJ knew they wouldn't find any evidence and he would be exonerated.

Given the timeline on Katie's body and how long she'd been dead, he was lucky that he'd been held up at the office for so long where there were security cameras everywhere. Which was all well and good, but then the police started asking questions about why someone would kill a girl in his apartment and why they'd leave a kidnapped baby there.

The less they said about David West the better. The last

thing they wanted was the police looking too closely at their lives.

JJ smiled as she watched Oskar reach out to hold Isabella. The baby clutched onto Lucia Koala-style, but eventually transferred to Oskar. And wonder of wonders, Isabella gave Oskar a wide smile. Right before — *oh no.*

The baby hiccupped and let out a torrent of vomit all over Oskar's face. JJ used her hand to cover her mouth before ducking out of the room to laugh.

She was laughing. Actual, *real* laughter. Poor Oskar. Poor Isabella. Poor thing probably had to burp. Who knew what kind of food Katie and that maniac had been giving her? The doctor said she was fine, but that baby was about to get spoiled rotten.

"How did I know I would find you out here laughing?"

JJ turned to face Jonas and leaned against the wall. "Because that shit was funny. Did you see the look on Oskar's face?"

"Why are you laughing at Oskar's woes and misfortune?"

"I'm not. But that was funny. She knows he's too uptight."

His lips twitched. He was clearly fighting a smile and

working hard on his stern face. She could see right through it. Eventually the chuckle broke through. "Yeah you're right. That shit was hilarious."

From the living room, they could hear Oskar cursing softly in German. It was funny, his German accent always became thicker when he was irritated or pissed off. But irritated or not, he used hushed tones for Isabella. "No, my darling. We talked about you saving spit up for your Uncle Rafe. He's the one who's truly deserving." Then he muttered under his breath. "Noah, your offspring is fucking with me."

The best part was every single man in that room, Noah, Rafe, Matthias, Ryan, and Dylan all muttered, "Language."

As if they all weren't bad about it themselves. Everyone was aware that Isabella was going to grow soon, which meant the usual sailor talk would have to be curbed. The crazy thing was JJ was worse than any of them. As Isabella's godmother she took it as her personal mantle to teach that girl how to curse properly.

JJ had already resigned herself to being the cause for Isabella's first appropriate use of the word fuck. Hey, they all had their cross to bear.

JJ slid her hand into Jonas's. "Are you sure you're okay?" She shook her head. "I can't imagine the scene you had to walk into today or how terrifying it must have been to face the possibility of jail."

He nodded. "I'm fine. I promise. Believe me, I've seen worse. Plus it was only jail, not prison. I had our lawyer. They processed me in, asked a couple of questions and watched the security footage then they processed me out. That's it. Nothing bad happened to me."

She nodded even as she held her breath and tried to hold back the sting of tears. She'd been terrified when Oskar had broken the news and worried about what could happen to him in there. "I just —" she sniffed. "I was worried."

He pulled her close and kissed her forehead. "Aww, come on now. I'm too pretty to be someone's jailhouse bitch."

She whacked him on the arm. "I'm being serious. You don't know David. He's crazy."

Jonas gently traced his fingers over her lips. "What I want to do right now is focus on you. I want to take your hand, lead you back into your room, strip these clothes off and sink into you. How does that sound for a plan?"

Well then, that was one way to shut her up. Because the moment he said the word sink, her core clenched and the hum of electricity danced on her skin. It had only been hours since she'd seen him, but she'd missed him.

It had been a long day. And with everything that had happened, she needed him. Now.

Jonas took JJ's hand and tugged her behind him. Once in the bedroom, he closed the door behind them and reached for her. But JJ knew what he was up to, and she wasn't going to be distracted.

She pushed him back by the shoulders. "No. You got arrested today. We know David could have killed you. I want you to care enough."

Jonas licked his bottom lip as he narrowed his gaze at her. She knew that look. It was all intensity and lust and need. "I know you were scared today. And I do care. A part of me was scared, too. But I know my team. There is always a way out. I trust that. Trust that no matter what, I'm not going down without a fight. You can't control the world around you, baby."

Her lip quivered. "Right now, I need control. I need to remind myself that you're alive, and that you're here, and that I didn't almost lose you today."

His gaze softened, and he leaned back against the door. "Okay. In that case, I'm all yours. Do your worst."

And she had every intention of it. "Stay there. Do not move. Do you understand?"

The grin he gave her was all cocky. But he nodded. "Yes, ma'am."

Hastily she tugged her blouse out of her skirt, unbuttoned the tiny row of buttons then shrugged it off her shoulders. Jonas's gaze homed in, and he turned that laser focus to her breasts. With every movement, jostle, and wiggle, he licked his lips. "I know what you're looking at. You're only torturing yourself. It's gonna be a long night. Ready?"

"Woman, I just got out of the joint. My patience can only take so much before I jump you."

"Well in that case, I better get down to business." JJ slipped out of her skirt, leaving only her stockings and her shoes on. When she stepped over to him, he groaned low.

She began working on his shirt, her bare hands tracing the planes of his chest, and he hissed. "Woman, you're killing me."

"That's the plan. To show you what you've been missing all day. Teach you not to get arrested next time."

His chuckle was low as she slid his shirt off his shoulders, and pressed a kiss to his nipple. "Yeah, I don't really have much to do with that. See, what happened was—"

"Hush. I'm busy."

Jonas cleared his throat and then laid his head back against the door. "Yeah, I can see that.

When his shirt dropped to the floor with barely a sound, JJ kissed across his fine pecs, and then shifted down to kiss each of his ribs and over his abs, sinking lower onto her knees.

"Oh God. JJ. Jessica —"

"Sssh. Woman at work here. Try to focus."

"Fuck, I am focused. You're all I'm focused on. I just —"

She was in no mood to listen to him. She just unbuckled his pants and smirked at the designer belt buckle and the dark wash of the $300 jeans. Jesus Christ, the man loved clothes more than she did. Even his boxers were designer. But of course they would be, because this, her big man, this was Jonas. All of him.

Once free, his cock bobbed in front of her face, fully erect, completely at attention, and begging for mercy. "My, my, someone has been missing me."

"I've just been to prison," he muttered through clenched teeth.

JJ chuckled. "I thought it was only jail?"

Jonas groaned when she teased her nails over the skin of his balls. "I need to get conjugal visits. JJ – fuck." He panted as she stroked him up and down gently, teasing the head then stroking down and cupping his balls.

"What were you saying?"

"Jessica, I need —" But he was done talking when she leaned forward and wrapped her lips around his dick. He stopped talking altogether. All that came from him were a series of moans and groans, as she worked him over with her tongue and her lips, and occasionally very gently with her teeth.

He dug his hands into her hair, and she relished every moment. The possession of it, the visceral nature of it. He was tugging on her hair. He was here. He was safe. He was *hers*.

He tried to pull her back, but she wasn't having it and

instead took him deeper, forcing the back of her throat to relax and defer to him.

"Oh my God, JJ," he growled. "I'm going to come."

Instead of drawing back like he wanted, she planted her hands on his hips and dug her nails into the top muscle of his ass and took him deeper.

His muscles tensed and bunched as he held her in place, and finally, he let go. When she eased back, Jonas's harsh pants tore out of his chest as he stared down at her. "Woman, Jesus."

"See, you like it when I'm in charge." She rose to her feet, intending to take her time with her stockings. He probably needed a minute, and in that time, she could grab a shower — before she knew what was happening, Jonas had her flat on her back in the bed.

He didn't bother removing her thong, but instead shoved the flimsy fabric aside and sank into her deep as he kissed her.

She gasped. "Jonas."

"You didn't think we were done did you? After all, I've just come home from prison. And I'm in my woman's bed.

We're gonna be here a while. So you might as well go ahead and get used to the size of me inside you."

The thing was JJ was so down for that.

It didn't take long. Two deep strokes, a quick flick of his thumb over her clit, his tongue sliding over hers, and she was flying.

JJ jumped with him into the abyss of bliss, finally letting go of the fear and the worry and the panic from today. He was home, he was safe, he was hers. And she was never letting go.

CHAPTER SEVEN

Over the next few days, Jonas tried to catch up on paperwork. Noah didn't want him out in the field, so he'd done as much at the penthouse as possible, burying himself in reports that he'd been too lazy to file last month. He figured if he was busy, he wouldn't have time to dwell on the ongoing investigation into Isabella's kidnapping and Katie's murder. But despite all his efforts, there was only so much paperwork he could do. And when he got JJ from work each day, it took all the energy he had to keep a smile on his face for her sake.

Not that it fooled her. JJ was just as on-edge as he was. And he spent each night staring at the ceiling as every detail of both cases scrolled through his mind.

There was something he was missing, and he was desperate to find it. JJ hadn't been sleeping any better. She tried to be quiet so he wouldn't know she was awake, but her breathing gave her away. His baby didn't know it, but she actually snored most of the time. A little tidbit he was saving to tell her at just the right time.

"You know, you could have taken a little time off."

Oskar's voice came from over Jonas's shoulder. He turned to look at him. His friend's usually stoic expression was twisted with worry.

Jonas sighed. The guys he worked with might be stone cold killers, but inside, they were all a bunch of gossipy, little old ladies. If he wasn't careful, they'd stage an intervention and force him to talk about his feelings.

"I'm fine. Like I told Noah this morning and Matthias this afternoon, I'm *fine*."

A woman going into the restroom they were guarding glanced at him in alarm. He pasted on a benign smile, and she glanced away quickly. Great. Now he was scaring the public.

"I'm just saying, no one would think less of you for needing a little time after everything that's happened."

Oskar's eyes scanned all the people walking up and down the hallway.

They were on the security detail for Sharla Winters, a B-list actress in town to do press for an upcoming movie. Normally Jonas avoided these sorts of details like the plague, but he'd taken the job at JJ's urging. It turned out his girl was a fan of Sharla's sorority house movies. Unfortunately, Sharla was nothing like the spunky, smart heroine of the movie series and was instead a spoiled brat who'd made this security detail unnecessarily difficult.

And besides, it was a job.

He couldn't allow Chamaeleon to run the show anymore. He'd spent the past few nights reassuring JJ that everything would be fine, and he was determined to keep that promise. His girl wanted everyone to believe she was hard as nails, but she'd been deeply affected by Isabella's kidnapping. He knew she still carried guilt over it and a deep-seated worry that David wasn't done screwing around with her loved ones.

Jonas didn't think it was over either, not that he'd share that thought with her. JJ needed to feel safe and protected, something he suspected she hadn't felt in a long time. That motherfucker had stolen her sense of safety, and Jonas was determined to be the one who restored it.

No matter what he had to do.

"She's been in there for a long time," Oskar muttered.

Jonas glanced at his watch and realized it had been almost ten minutes since Sharla had entered the restroom. Oskar had done a sweep before she went in but it was still odd. In this line of work you learned to trust your instincts, and his were ringing big time.

"I'm going in," Oskar growled, clearly feeling the same way.

Jonas sharpened his gaze on all of the people walking by. Only two women had entered after Sharla, both on the list of attendees at the event that they'd previously vetted.

But that doesn't mean someone wasn't in there already.

Jonas cursed, more certain as the minutes passed that something was wrong. Suddenly there was a loud shout and a crash against the door.

"Oskar!" He pushed against the bathroom door but there was something blocking it. He pushed harder and managed to squeeze through the opening in the door.

Oskar was on the ground right inside the door, writhing in pain. As much as he wanted to stop and check on his friend, protocol dictated that he secure the area first.

He drew his weapon and swept past the small sitting area and into the actual restroom. One of the faucets was running, and the small window over the last stall was open.

"Fuck! How the hell did we miss that?"

He would have sworn there were no windows or doors leading out of this restroom when they'd done their earlier walkthrough of the building.

In the last stall, he also found Sharla standing on the toilet looking terrified. "Is it safe to come out? Oskar told me to hide in here."

Jonas nodded and then immediately raced back to the sitting area at the mention of Oskar. His friend was red in the face and didn't look to be breathing.

"Sharla, call 911!"

Jonas dropped to the ground and put his fingers on Oskar's pulse. Steady but getting fainter.

"Tell them I'm starting CPR," he called over his shoulder,

hoping like hell that Sharla would follow directions for once.

He started chest compressions, then pinched Oskar's nostrils, tipped his chin up, and started breathing for him. After a moment he listened, and when he didn't hear breathing, started chest compressions again. Just when he was about to pinch his nostrils again, Oskar leaned to the side and coughed violently. One of his huge arms swung out and swatted Jonas so hard he fell over.

"God damn, if you wanted to kiss me that bad, all you had to do was ask."

Jonas was so relieved he could only laugh. "That's what I get for trying to save your life, asshole."

Oskar struggled to sit up. "Where is she? That crazy bitch hit me with a taser!"

Jonas shook his head. "Whoever she was, she's gone. When I came in, the window was open, the window that *wasn't there* when we did our sweep earlier, and you were on the ground."

Sharla appeared at his shoulder. "Why would someone attack him though? That chick didn't even look at me. What kind of deranged fan is that?"

Jonas had to refrain from rolling his eyes. Sharla seemed disappointed that her "fan" hadn't attempted to hurt her. God, he was done protecting the Hollywood set. Completely self-absorbed, all of them.

"She has a point," Oskar rasped, one hand pressed to his chest. "If Sharla was the target, why didn't she attack once I was down?"

His mind spinning, Jonas stood and walked back into the restroom. The magic window still hung open, and the sound of traffic and voices floated in. As he got closer, he could see where the drywall had been ripped away to reveal the glass beneath. Whoever had planned this had done their research and had known that window was there. Someone with that level of precision wouldn't allow a prime opportunity to attack pass them by.

Which meant they'd gotten to their intended target.

"Sharla wasn't who they were after," he mumbled.

After coming in from work, JJ waved absently over her shoulder at Matthias, who'd picked her up.

"Hey, JJ! How were things today?" Lucia came out of her room, Isabella bundled in her arms.

The sight of her goddaughter snuggled safely in her friend's arms brought a lump to her throat.

JJ smiled brightly. "Great! I think we're catching up finally." She backed up toward her room. Desperation clawed up from her throat, making her feel like she was on the verge of screaming. "I'm just going to go drop my stuff off."

Lucia watched her with knowing eyes. "Okay. I made lasagna for dinner. I'll save you a plate."

JJ smiled her thanks and hurried into her room. She closed the door and for the first time all day, allowed the smile on her face to drop.

"Oh thank god," she whispered, resting her head against the door. The cool wood against her skin grounded her and calmed the raging surge of emotions bubbling just beneath the surface.

It was harder than she'd expected to keep it together and pretend to be fine. Especially with both Jonas and Lucia watching her like a hawk. A few saucy comments had fooled Matthias, and he'd pretty much left her alone during the day, even though she'd been aware of him in the corner of her office typing furiously on his laptop. But Matthias was a quiet sort himself and didn't expect, or want, conversation.

Fooling those closest to her was another story. Each night, she spent some time with Lucia and had even held Isabella a few times. But it was getting harder and harder to make small talk and pretend to be relaxed when inside she was shredding into a million pieces.

How could everyone else be so calm when at this very moment, David was out there, probably watching and plotting his next move? How could they breathe knowing he could attack at any moment?

They don't know him like you do, that's why.

JJ shuddered, thoughts of David making her instantly wish for a shower. Her hands tightened around the straps of her handbag. It was relatively new, a white and red striped tote bag that she'd loved as soon as she saw it. Had David been watching even then? Perhaps followed her around the store as she'd contemplated between the available bags? She had no idea how long he'd been watching and waiting to make his move.

Would she ever feel safe again?

Overcome, she slung the bag across the room. It skittered over the bed before falling over the other side with a thump. Enraged, JJ yanked at the bracelets on her arm and threw those, too. Part of her wanted to strip everything away, as if ridding herself of the pretty clothes David had always loved to see her in could purge him from her life. She tore at her blouse, buttons popping off and landing on the floor, before pushing her skirt down. Tears streamed down her face as she stumbled while trying to get the skirt down her legs.

"Get it off. Get it off," she mumbled, frantic to be free. Hands settled on her arms, and she shrieked in surprise. "Don't touch me! Stay away from me."

"Whoa, baby! It's me."

Jonas's voice penetrated through the fog of panic, but JJ was too far gone to stop. She pulled at her bra, shuddering when strong arms wrapped around her tight, holding her in place.

"Stop, baby girl. You're scratching yourself. Just hold on."

JJ struggled weakly in his arms before all at once, her energy drained and she collapsed against his chest. She let out a ragged breath, wrapping her legs around his waist as he carried her over to the bed. When she felt the mattress beneath her, she curled up in a ball. After a moment, she opened one eye and watched as Jonas shed his clothes too.

"Scoot over, I'm coming in."

His husky voice brought a smile to her face. JJ had to give it to him, no matter how strangely she behaved, Jonas just rolled with it. The man had the patience of a saint, but how long could that last? Especially when he realized that she hadn't been completely honest with him. It was only after staring at him that she saw the strain on his face, the lines around his eyes and mouth that no one else would probably notice.

Something was wrong.

"What happened?"

Jonas turned his head toward her. His heavy sigh carried a wealth of meaning. "Someone came after Oskar today with a taser. They didn't go after the client at all."

He didn't say anything else, but JJ could read the worry in his voice. This wasn't just a random thing. Just as she'd suspected, David had decided how to extract his pound of flesh.

Through the people she cared about.

"He's never going to stop, is he?" JJ whispered.

Strong fingers gripped her chin and forced her to hold still. JJ kept her eyes squeezed shut for a minute but she couldn't hide from this forever. When she opened them, Jonas was watching her with the gentlest look in his eyes.

"It's not your fault." He leaned forward and pressed a soft kiss to her forehead. "He's going to make a mistake eventually. Then we'll take him out."

JJ didn't bother asking what he meant by that. Over time, she'd clued in to the alternative methods Noah and his whole crew employed when dealing with the various scumbags they encountered. Once upon a time, she'd have been bothered by it. Before she knew how many people in this world didn't play by the rules. Now if given the opportunity, she would take David out herself.

"You're only saying that because you don't know him. You don't know what he's capable of and how deep this obsession runs."

"So tell me," Jonas countered, his eyes holding hers. "Tell me whatever it is you're so afraid will change things."

Of course he'd known all along that she was holding back. How silly that she'd ever thought she could fool him. For so long, she'd kept Jonas at a distance with harsh words, but that was probably because she'd sensed that once she let him in, there would be no more secrets. She was going to have to reveal every layer of her shame for everyone to dissect and judge.

Maybe it was time. It was her sins coming home to roost. And if she had to bare her soul to clean the slate, that would be her penance.

"Okay. I'll tell you everything. But it has to be all at once. I can't retell it multiple times. I just don't have it in me."

His hand was still tangled in her hair, rubbing a gentle circle. JJ closed her eyes and savored his touch. After this story came out, there wouldn't be any more soft kisses or comfort from Jonas. She'd be lucky if she had a place to stay.

"I'll tell the others. We'll call a meeting so you can tell everyone at once. Once it's out there, maybe we can end this."

JJ nodded. "We can end this."

It would be the end of everything. On impulse, she sprang forward, plastering herself to him, locking their lips together and running her fingers through his hair. Jonas groaned deep in his throat, his hands automatically gripping her ass, kneading and caressing. JJ shuddered, licking into his mouth before biting his bottom lip hard.

"Jesus, you're killing me."

If they had more time, she'd have pulled him into the bed and had her way with him one more time. But now that she'd made the decision, it was time to follow through before she lost her nerve. So JJ sat back and took a deep breath. Jonas watched her carefully before pulling out his phone. As she watched him typing out a message, JJ put her hand on his.

"Tell them Rafe needs to be there, too."

Jonas frowned. "Why does he need to be there?"

"He just does. This involves him, too."

Jonas's brow furrowed and he held her eyes for a moment before nodding sharply.

CHAPTER EIGHT

"Okay we're all here, now. JJ, this is your show."

Jonas knew he sounded like an asshole, but ever since those words had left JJ's lips, 'this involves him too,' he'd been on edge. He glanced at Rafe from the corner of his eyes. When he'd texted Noah with the request for a group meeting, including Rafe, he wasn't the only one who thought it strange.

Rafe worked with them, but it was relatively recent. He did the jobs Noah assigned without complaint, and there was no denying he was a lethal bastard, but he usually wasn't included when they discussed company business of any kind. Not that Rafe seemed to care. Jonas didn't get the impression the man enjoyed spending time around other people, anyway. The only ones who brought out any sign of humanity in him were his little sister and his grandmother.

Speaking of, Lucia seemed to sense the strange tension in the room as well because she hadn't left Rafe's side since he'd arrived. Rafe put an arm around her and she leaned into him.

"Yes, I did ask for this meeting." JJ glanced at him and smiled tremulously.

Jonas smiled back, rewarded when the haunted look in her eyes receded slightly.

"I need to tell you about how I met David."

Noah leaned forward. "Back when you and Lucia were teenagers."

"Yes. It was right after..." she glanced over at Rafe, "you know."

Rafe stood up straighter. "You met him right after I disappeared?"

JJ nodded. "He saved me from these guys who were hassling me on the street. At the time, it seemed so romantic. Like he was protecting me. We started dating soon after that."

She fell silent, and Jonas reached over to hold her hand. There was obviously more to this story than boy meets girl, boy becomes stalker. JJ had been tense ever since she'd asked him to call this meeting, and her request to see Rafe had definitely put him on edge, too. Jonas wasn't too proud to admit that he didn't want that guy anywhere near his girl. He wasn't normally the jealous type, but Rafe could probably trigger that instinct in any guy. Hell, he wasn't too proud to admit that he couldn't best the guy in a fight, either. The only one who might have a shot was Noah, and that was because Rafe had trained him for years.

"David was really nice to me at first. He took me to dinner and listened while I told him about everything going on in my life. Rafe had just died and everything was crazy."

Lucia sniffled. "I can't believe I didn't know anything about this."

JJ walked over to Lucia. "You were grieving. And I didn't want to say anything that would make it worse. David was an outsider, so I could talk to him without bringing up any bad memories. Or at least, that's what I thought. I was trying to be there for you and Nonna, but it was a lot to process for a teenage girl. I had never known someone who'd died before. Especially not someone…"

She glanced over at Rafe and swallowed. "Not someone I loved."

Jonas blinked. When he looked over at Rafe, he saw that the other man was also frozen in place.

"What?" He asked what everyone in the room was thinking.

JJ put a hand to her cheek, which was slowly turning pink. "I had a crush on Rafe." She said it so softly that Jonas could barely hear her. But he knew Noah had heard because of his friend's soft intake of breath.

"Oh shit," Oskar muttered.

"Anyway," JJ continued loudly, "David listened to me, and he told me about losing his father years before. We bonded and before long, I was spending more and more time with him. Too much time. He didn't want me to hang out with anyone else. If I wanted to go see Lucia, he would follow me and wait outside. He'd walk me to and from school and if I was even a minute late, he'd accuse me of staying behind to flirt with the boys in my class. It started to feel like I was in prison."

Rafe and Noah exchanged glances and Rafe said, "That's straight out of the ORUS playbook. Establish a rapport with the target and then isolate them. Do you think this was Orion checking up? Maybe he suspected that I was still around and was using JJ to confirm?"

"It's possible," Noah admitted. "Although it would have been more likely that he'd go after Lucia."

"I don't think that's what he was after," JJ said slowly. "David asked a lot of questions about Rafe, but not like he doubted his death."

Rafe narrowed his eyes. "What kind of questions?"

JJ instantly blushed bright red. "Just what kind of stuff you liked. Whether I saw you a lot when I visited Lucia. Then other things." She fidgeted with the edge of her shirt.

Lucia put her arm around her. "It's okay."

JJ kept her eyes on the floor as she continued. "He wanted to know if I'd ever kissed Rafe. He was obsessed. If I ever brought his name up, it enraged David. He knew how I felt about him and wanted to prove he was the better choice. Any time a guy looked at me on the street, David would try to fight him. Like he wanted to prove how strong he was. Then he started asking me to call him that. When we... you know."

Everyone shifted uncomfortably. Noah looked like he'd rather be anywhere else but somehow got it together to ask what was necessary.

"He wanted you to call him Rafe's name during sex."

"Um, yeah. Uh huh." JJ put a hand over her heart and rubbed. "He started getting rougher with me and I got scared enough to leave. But he was waiting for me after school the next day. That was the first time he hit me."

Lucia pulled her close. "And I wasn't there for you. I'm so sorry."

JJ leaned her head against Lucia's shoulder. "It wasn't your fault."

"But still, you went through this all alone."

JJ swiped at her eyes. "I was afraid to tell anyone. He controlled what I wore and where I went, and he made sure I knew there was no escape. He said if I ever left him again, he would hurt my mom. He couldn't get to Lucia since Noah was always around, but I still worried that he'd try something. I figured he was going to eventually kill me. Nothing I did seemed to satisfy him. Then all of a sudden, he was just gone."

Noah narrowed his eyes. "That must have been when Orion sent him overseas. Do you think he found out what was going on?"

Rafe shrugged. "It's possible. ORUS agents aren't supposed to form any attachments. If Orion caught wind that Chamaeleon had a girlfriend, especially one connected to me, he'd have squashed that shit quickly."

"But why bring him back?" Jonas wondered.

"Ian didn't know about any of this. He wasn't in charge back then, remember? It's been almost seven years," Noah mused. "Even if all this was documented somewhere, no one would think a relationship he had with a teenager years ago would be a threat anymore."

Rafe put his hands on his head. "I'm going to kill that fucker."

"Get in line," Jonas growled. He flexed the fingers that had been clenched in a fist for the past ten minutes. He'd thought there was nothing worse than hearing about how his woman had fantasized about Rafe, but hearing how she'd feared for her life with nowhere to turn was even worse.

Not that he hadn't been motivated to find the fucker before, but now he wanted to find him and cause him pain. David West was going to know the same terror he'd put JJ through for months.

———

JJ had reached the limits of her endurance. She pulled away from Lucia, squeezing her friend's arm gently. There was going to be a long gab session in their future, she was sure. Lucia was still digesting everything she'd heard today, but JJ had no doubt she was going to be in for it later. It was a huge secret she'd kept from her friend for years.

"We'll talk later, okay?"

Lucia nodded. "There's plenty of time for that. Right now, I think you have one very patient man to explain a few things to. And for what it's worth, he really loves you."

JJ's eyes met Jonas's over her friend's shoulder. He watched her with a burning intensity that under any other circumstances, she would have thought was desire. But then his eyes swung over to where Rafe stood, and the spark shifted into something closer to rage.

Uh-oh.

"Yeah, I think maybe Jonas and I need to have a chat." More like, she needed to get to Jonas before he started something with Rafe. She'd heard from Lucia what had happened the last time Rafe had fought the guys. He'd singlehandedly managed to injure half the team. The last thing she wanted was anyone fighting over her.

Rafe ducked out of the room and by the time JJ looked for Jonas again, he was gone. Her pulse sped up as she glanced around. Oskar was across the room talking to Matthias. Noah stood behind them, waiting for Lucia. Ryan and Dylan had left already. *Oh shit.*

"I'll see you later." JJ hugged Lucia again and then walked out into the entryway. Rafe and Jonas stood glaring at each other. It brought to mind two lions facing off in the wild. No one spoke or turned when she approached.

JJ stepped in between them and took Jonas's hand. "Can I talk to you for a second?"

A beat later, his eyes met hers. His nostrils flared briefly, but he nodded. "Yeah. I'll be there in a second."

"Right now, actually."

She tugged on his hand, not even acknowledging Rafe. If she so much as glanced in his direction, the tentative cease fire between the two would probably go up in smoke. JJ mentally rolled her eyes. Juggling the egos of all these alpha males was like tap dancing around dynamite.

It took a few tugs, but Jonas finally allowed her to pull him back into the living room. All JJ could hope for was that Rafe would leave, otherwise she'd have to worry about the two men getting into it all night. Although she doubted Rafe really wanted to stick around. It had been beyond humiliating to have to say those things in front of him and everyone else. Embarrassment flared again. The poor man was probably going to ask Lucia to start coming to him when he wanted to see his sister.

The living room was empty, everyone having gone back to their various rooms.

"So, I figured maybe we should talk."

Jonas shrugged. "We don't need to talk. You were right that hearing the whole story helped. David's behavior has been erratic and unpredictable this whole time, but understanding what makes him tick will only help us."

JJ's mouth fell open. He was talking like this was any other standard case and the only thing he was concerned with was chasing down a target. Of all the reactions she'd expected him to have, this wasn't one of them. It couldn't have been fun to hear his girlfriend admit to fantasizing about one of his coworkers during sex. Especially a co-worker who'd once hurt him so badly.

"I hope it does help," she said finally, at a loss as to what else to say. If he didn't want to talk about all the embarrassing stuff she'd said, then she definitely wasn't going to bring it up.

"Okay, so maybe we should just stay in and take it easy tonight. We can watch something on Netflix, and I'll make us some sandwiches," JJ suggested.

Jonas nodded. "Sure. We can make some popcorn and chill."

They were interrupted by Noah and JJ stepped back to allow the men to talk. Jonas gestured for her to wait and followed Noah from the room, so JJ figured she'd get started preparing their little picnic.

She'd been stressing ever since she'd asked him to call for the meeting, sure that once it was over, Jonas would be annoyed with her. Not because of what happened years ago, but because she'd kept it from them all. Also, he was a typical guy, competitive and slightly possessive. Not enough to be a problem but she knew he didn't like the idea of sharing any part of her. It would only be natural for him to wonder if any of her earlier feelings had survived her teenage crush.

Especially now that Rafe was back in her life. But all she felt for him was a brotherly affection, similar to how she'd viewed him before her crush took hold. Lucia was thrilled beyond reason to have her brother back, and JJ was so happy for her and Nonna. But his reappearance hadn't changed her feelings at all. Jonas was the only man she wanted. After having her trust shattered by David, it had taken a long time before she'd felt ready to be vulnerable with a man again. She couldn't have done that with anyone but Jonas. No one else had been willing to spar with her and endure the barbs to get to the real Jessica beneath the attitude.

"I'll have turkey on mine." Jonas appeared at her elbow. His forehead was crinkled the way it always was when he was worried about something.

JJ glanced behind him. Noah stood at the edge of the kitchen watching them. She couldn't decode the expression on his face, but he glanced at Jonas one more time before he turned to leave.

"Is everything okay with Noah?" she finally asked.

Jonas grimaced. "Noah needs to mind his own business."

Whoa. She wasn't going there. JJ was under no impression that the guys always agreed. Noah was their boss and he wasn't exactly a tactful guy. But she'd never heard Jonas say even one negative word about his friend and boss before today. *Before you pushed him to the edge.*

Wordlessly, she reached for the sliced turkey, making sandwiches for them both. Jonas worked quietly beside her, putting the food on a tray and then putting some popcorn in the microwave. She opened the refrigerator and pulled out a coke for him and a Dr. Pepper for herself.

Jonas's eyes landed on the sodas as she put them on the tray. "Dr. Pepper," he murmured.

JJ stilled. "Yeah. It's my favorite. I've been drinking it since I was a teenager."

His eyes flared. "Rafe drinks Dr. Pepper. It's the only one I've ever seen him drink."

Her heart sank. She thought back to when she was a young girl, watching Rafe mainline Dr. Pepper like it was water. She'd started drinking it too, thinking maybe he'd notice that she liked the same thing he did.

How had she forgotten that?

JJ licked her lips nervously as she turned to face Jonas. "Jonas. Look it's not like—"

His voice, as icy as steel, cut her off. "Be quiet."

Gone was his usual smug smile or cocky smirk. She could see the muscles of his jaw working as he clenched his teeth together. Holding her hand tight, Jonas turned down the hall and stalked into one of the bedrooms, kicking the door shut behind them.

"Jonas, that was a really long time ago. I don't have a thing for Rafe now. You have to understand that."

Jonas said nothing, just narrowed his gaze at the mention

of Rafe's name. He backed her up and with a few short strides, he laid her on the bed, following her down.

With a muffled growl, he scooted them up toward the headboard then dragged her over him so she straddled his lap. Easing up his grip on her hair, he gently massaged her scalp until she was nearly limp and pliant in his arms. She could feel his anger coursing through him, but at the same time she knew she could trust him. Knew that he wouldn't hurt her.

When he brought her head down for a kiss, JJ couldn't help but moan. His tongue slid over hers easily and she whimpered. Jonas nipped at her bottom lip before sucking on it gently. Her lips tingled, the pleasure flowing white hot through her, and she wondered if she might be able to come just from his kisses. And if not, the delicious rub of his cock against her sensitive flesh would do the trick.

One of his big hands gripped her ass, gently rocking her into him as he devoured her mouth. With every rock of their hips together, they both made this satisfied, muffled *mmph* sound. As if that was exactly what hit the spot, what they both needed.

Holy hell. She was close and so far all he'd done was kiss her. But it was more than that. The tension between them was so thick, winding tighter around them with each moment.

She wasn't an idiot. She knew there was still a lot of underlying tension with Rafe. After all, Rafe had tried to kill him before. But she'd had no idea that he would respond like this. Any feelings she'd ever had for Rafe were a schoolgirl crush. That crush didn't come anywhere close to what they shared. Not even close. But how the hell did she drive that message home?

At that moment, he was acting like a caveman with a need to mark her... not that she minded. She trusted him. He wasn't going to hurt her. She just didn't want him thinking that any part of her wanted anyone else.

Jonas tore his lips off of hers, panting as his gaze bore into her eyes. With a muffled curse, he flipped them so that he lay on top of her, his hips fitting in that space she made just for him between her thighs. "You are the most beautiful woman I've ever laid my eyes on. And you're *mine*. If you're gonna tell anyone to sit and spin it'll be me. Is that clear?"

JJ nodded as she reached for him, making this little mewling sound in the back of her throat. Was that really her? Sounding needy and desperate? "Okay, Jonas. Just—"

But it was like he couldn't hear her. Against her skin, he whispered, "Did you know how many times I used to dream about touching you? About all the ways I could make you scream my name?"

"Jonas—"

He kissed behind her ear as he rocked his cock against her heat. "I used to spend a lot of time in the shower every morning and night thinking about you. About how you'd taste, how your breasts would look soaped up. About how bad I wanted to lick you everywhere. And when I'd take my cock into my hand, I'd pretend it was you sliding your fingers over me, making me feel good. I'd pretend you were squeezing just how I like, bringing me to my knees. I'd pretend you were slick, and wet, and ready for me, begging me to make love to you." He nipped at her skin. "And every time I came, it was your name I'd call."

JJ arched her back. Her brain offered up the mental image of him stroking his thick erection, squeezing tight as he pulled the skin taut and groaned out her name. "D-do you always use my name when you're touching yourself?"

He rocked his hips into her as he kissed the column of her throat. "Yes. Most of the time I imagine you're there, touching me. Wrapping those gorgeous lips of yours around me. Sucking me as you blink up at me, adoringly. And while I'm sliding into your mouth, I'm telling you all the dirty things I'm going to do to you."

Dirty talk—she was a fan. If this was what happened every time Jonas got pissed off, she'd maybe have to push his buttons more often.

Everything he said to her just made her wetter, especially when he coupled it with rubbing his cock just over her clit. "What kind of dirty things?"

He pulled back a little so he could look at her. A slow, devilish smile played across his lips. "Judging by the curiosity in your voice, you want me to tell you every dirty detail, don't you? You want me talking to you all dirty, telling you how I'm going to work my way backwards with you."

Oh God, so close, the tingles spread over her skin and she arched into him, begging him silently for more friction. "Yes, Jonas."

"You want me to tell you how you suck my cock so good,

taking me deep, using your tongue against me, making me beg."

"Mmmm." More, she needed more.

"Then just as I'm about to explode, I pull out before you can make me come and I slide my cock bare inside your hot little pussy. Inch by inch, you cling onto me, milking me, begging me to come."

Jesus. Why did the idea of him making love to her without a condom sound so hot? She'd always used condoms. But with Jonas, the idea took root and flourished. What would it feel like?

"Then you fuck me so good with your slick wet, heat, and I make you come over and over again."

Oh hell yes. She wanted that with him. More than she'd ever wanted anyone in her life.

"But I won't be done, sweetheart. As you already know my rule is ladies first. Then second. And then if I'm lucky, maybe third before I come. But I still won't be done with you. Because you need to know I am the only one who can make you come like that."

He shifted and slid off of her to make quick work of her shoes, tossing them over his shoulders. They landed with thuds somewhere by the door. He was impatient with her dress, yanking and tugging quickly until it was somewhere in a corner.

He took his time watching her, paying particular attention to her breasts. When he leaned back over her, he reached behind her and unsnapped her bra one-handed. The motion was so quick, she had to laugh. "I see you've had some practice with that."

He smirked as he leaned back over her. "Only a little." Jonas kissed her again before sliding his lips to her jaw, his hands rising up to lock with hers.

JJ rocked her hips upward and reached for him, sliding her fingers through his hair. "Please hurry."

"I'll get there when I get there." He said with a harsh chuckle. "But not before I remind you of who's in your bed. Of who exactly it is that loves you. Who is about to be inside you." He grazed along the column of her throat even as his hips rocked into hers, pressing gently. Teasing her with the ridge of his erection.

JJ bit her lip. "Fuck. I know who's about to be inside me. Your name starts with a J right?"

He chuckled even as he smacked her ass. "Naughty thing.

So you know, after we make love, I'm going to use my fingers, I'll slide them inside you and over your skin. I'll find your G-spot and touch it just right. Just enough to make you come again. I know you'll be sensitive, but it's going to feel so good."

He sped up his movements, his hips rolling into hers. She rose to meet him, arching her back, begging him to rub her where she needed. His lips skimmed over her skin, across her collarbone to her breast. His words alone were driving her nuts. But coupled with his lips, his hands intertwined with hers, she was ready to explode.

"I want to make love to every inch of you. Especially these. But tonight, when I'm done stroking you with my fingers, I'm going to taste you. I'll put my mouth on you and lick you until you melt." When his lips reached the top swell of her breasts, he moaned. "Jesus, you are so pretty. So full, so soft."

His lips brushed her nipple ever so slightly. The motion sent a spear of need directly to her core. Next he used just his teeth, raking gently. He was careful to keep his full weight off of her. His teeth felt so good and she wondered if it was possible to die from anticipation. When he laved her distended nipple with his tongue and then wrapped his lips around her, JJ held on for her life. With tug after deep tug, he sucked on her.

It didn't take much, she was so tightly wound. But it was the secondary pleasure when he teased her other nipple with his thumb that sent her over the edge. She came hard and fast, her whole body shaking. "Jonas. Oh my God."

He pulled back with a satisfied grin. "That's one." His clothes went quickly and he took far less care with them than he'd taken with hers, except when he snagged a condom out of his wallet. The only other time he slowed was when he worked her panties down her legs.

He hooked his thumbs into the elastic and ripped. JJ gasped, when he licked his lips as she placed her sex directly in front of him. Jonas kissed down her thighs and her calves to her feet before tossing what was left of the flimsy garment over his head.

He ripped open the condom and slid it on before settling between her thighs. "Look at me, JJ."

As if she could look anywhere else. Even though she felt like a limp noodle, she still wanted more.

One hand teasing the hair at his nape, the other tracing his pecs, she canted her hips up. "Jonas, more."

His voice might have been teasing, but she could see the tension in him as his arms shook. He was having a hard time with control.

Would talking to him drive him as crazy as it drove her? He lined his erection up with her opening and she whispered, "I want to know what this feels like bare. Just you and me, nothing between us. Do you think you'll like that?"

He stared down at her, lips slightly parted. "What?"

"It would be a first. I want to know what it feels like to have you come inside me."

He rocked into her in one deep stroke, her name on his tongue. He cursed low and deep, a long drawn out "Fuuuuck."

Jonas slid in and retreated, adjusting their position so she sat on his lap. Oh yes, he hit so deep like this. Their motions were a frenzy of skin, lips and hands. There wasn't a part of him he didn't touch her with. Body and soul.

Her second orgasm was stronger than the first, but with a slow build. Once the fire took hold, there was no stopping it and she exploded in his arms, a scream tearing out of her chest.

Jonas was right behind her. His hips bucked as he came, and he gripped her ass tightly as his muscles corded and his teeth clenched. JJ wrapped her arms around him, holding tight. He was hers. *And she was his.*

———

He was acting like a jealous prick. Jonas knew it, but he didn't give two shits right at the moment. He had spent half the night making sure she knew she was his. It had been part seduction, part distraction, part branding.

With everything she'd been through lately, he should let her rest. But then his brain would remind him that she used to fantasize about Rafe, and then he'd need to brand her all over again.

You're acting like a moron. You love her. And she loves you. You can protect her. But that didn't make the gnawing annoyance and fear in his gut dissipate.

She wiggled in her sleep, and he groaned as her bare ass slid over his dick.

Why couldn't he get enough of her? More importantly

why was he acting like such a crazy man? *Because you've never loved anyone before.* Not like this anyway. It was more than just her schoolgirl crush on Rafe. The whole David West situation was gnawing at him. He hated that that psychopath had ever been near her let alone put hands on her. He wanted to erase that memory from her mind as well.

All he wanted to do was wrap his arms around her and keep her safe. He wanted to fuck her too... *again.* And again. But he liked just holding her. Watching the play of early morning sunlight on her hair. He listened to her breathing. *Sap.* How in the world was her breathing sexy? Easy. Everything about her was sexy.

She rotated her hips again, and he slid his hands down the flat of her belly to the juncture of her thighs. Even sleepy, she slid them open for him, welcoming his touch. She was so responsive. When he slid his fingers through her smooth lips, they both gasped. Him at how soft she was; her at his penetration. He whispered against her nape, her soft curls tickling his nose. "Touching you is an addiction now."

"Good."

He nipped her neck as he slid another finger into her,

penetrating deeper, his fingers growing slicker. She hooked her leg over his and slid her hands behind her to wind into his hair. Fuck, he loved it when she tugged a little. She was so hot. So ready.

He removed his fingers and she whimpered, but then he slid his fingers over her lips. And when she tentatively licked them, he almost came. Staring at her pink tongue, he slid his cock along her slit, fighting the urge to sink into her deep. He'd never had sex without a condom. And he wasn't starting now. But her words from yesterday rang in his skull and he just had to feel her.

When she sucked his fingers into her mouth, he cursed. "Shit, Jessica. I could explode just from watching you."

She released him and turned slightly, meeting his gaze directly. "I want you to."

His smile spread slowly and he kissed her lightly. Her taste on her lips was enough to have the base of his spine tingling. So close. So damn close.

His cock twitched against her folds. She scooted her hips back, sliding her slick pussy over the length of him. His already tenuous control snapped then, and he firmly hooked her leg over his, sliding in to the hilt. God, that was good. "Jessica..." Her name tripped reverently off his tongue. She was so tight and so warm around him that he lost another piece of himself. And as he took them both slowly over the edge of ecstasy, he knew he was never going to let anyone hurt her.

CHAPTER TEN

When he woke again, Jonas felt like roadkill.

He groaned and rolled over, pressing a hand to the forehead that was currently splitting and felt like it was partially detached from the rest of his body. Damn getting old was hell. He used to be able to engage in an all-night sexathon without waking feeling used up and dried out. Obviously, not any longer. And if the soft whimpers coming from the other side of the bed were any indication, JJ wasn't feeling much better than he was.

"Oh god, is it morning already? I have to go to work!" JJ screeched.

He clapped his hands over his ears. "No, you don't. It's Saturday."

She sighed in relief and dropped her head back down to the pillow. It occurred to Jonas that he wasn't actually sure what day it was, but it was worth the lie if it kept her from screaming in his ear. Considering how much she worked, he figured she had to have some sick days coming, even if it was a workday.

What time was it? It took him a while to gather the energy to sit up, but once he did, he instantly regretted it.

That was it. He was buying a new head. This one was officially broken. Not that he regretted it. All he had to do was think about how hot, open, and responsive JJ had been last night, and he was hard as a rock again. He hadn't even thought his dick was capable of filling again after putting in five impressive performances. Jonas smiled in satisfaction. He might be tired, but he still had it, damn it.

"Did everybody hear me screaming last night?" JJ asked, almost as if she could hear his thoughts.

Her voice was small, and it instantly wiped away the prior satisfaction Jonas had been feeling. Yes, he'd wanted to brand her as his and yes, he'd wanted the whole world to know it. But in the midst of his alpha-male posturing, he'd lost sight of how it would make JJ feel to have her best friend and the guys she had to see everyday hearing her scream her head off.

Way to go asshole. You just embarrassed her when you're supposed to be showing her why she belongs with you.

"I'm sure everyone was asleep," he lied.

"Right. Everyone slept through me screeching like a banshee and moaning your name. God!"

JJ pressed the pillow to her face and fell back to the bed dramatically. Despite everything, Jonas found himself smiling at her antics. This was what he'd dreamed of, sharing this intimate time with her when her hair wasn't done and they both had creases in their faces from the pillowcases. He loved that he knew what she looked like when she woke up and the husky timbre of her voice when she was fresh from dreaming. No one else got to see her like that.

"I'm not going out there. I'll just stay here."

Jonas chuckled. "All day?"

"Yes. All day. I can have my food shipped. Hopefully Adriana will let me work remotely from now on."

It took a lot of cajoling and some sneakily placed kisses but Jonas was finally able to convince JJ to leave the sanctuary of the covers and venture out for breakfast. They'd both burned a lot of calories the night before. Plus, he figured they might as well get the good-natured ribbing coming from Noah and the guys over with. When JJ realized it was going to be the same teasing they were used to, she'd get over her shyness. Hell, she'd probably tell them to stop being pervs and listening. JJ was a ball buster and he loved her that way.

"I'm so hungry," JJ moaned as they walked down the hallway after a hot shower. "I hope Oskar hasn't eaten all the bacon."

Before Jonas could answer, they rounded the corner into the kitchen and stopped in their tracks. Ryan stood in the kitchen pouring a cup of coffee, but everyone else was sitting around the long oak table in the dining area.

Including Rafe.

"Good morning!" Lucia called. "I saved you some pancakes and bacon."

JJ smiled gratefully at her friend, but Jonas could already see the pink inching up her cheeks. She rarely blushed, and most of the times he'd seen her do it had been over the last few days.

Because of Rafe. She blushed for that bastard.

"Thank you. We're both starving." Jonas turned to Lucia, determined to ignore the other side of the room. Until he heard a round of masculine laughter and his eyes were pulled over again.

Rafe smirked.

"I bet. Yo, we get it. She's yours and you're the only one who can make her scream your name. But I don't think they heard her in New Jersey."

JJ blushed bright red and dropped the plate of food she was holding on the counter with a clatter. "I'm not hungry."

"Rafe!" Lucia yelled.

Rafe looked slightly chagrined. "Come on blondie, I was just joking," he yelled after JJ's retreating form. A few seconds later, a door in the hallway closed firmly.

Jonas was across the room before he had a chance to think, and only Oskar stepping in his way stopped his momentum.

"Fuck you, man. What are you even doing here?"

"I work here, remember? And my sister lives here." Rafe drawled lazily, as if the entire situation amused him.

That only infuriated Jonas more. The bastard acted like everything was a joke. Especially considering how long he'd been gone from his sister's life. He thought he could flit in and out of his family's life with no consequences? Jonas didn't even know the whole story, but he was furious about Rafe's actions on Lucia's behalf. She'd mourned her brother for years.

"Your sister living here didn't seem to influence your decisions at any other time in your life," he pointed out.

Like a black cloud had just passed, the temperature in the room dropped a few degrees. Rafe stood slowly. "You don't know what the fuck you're talking about."

"Why don't you come over here and tell me then," Jonas sneered.

Rafe laughed. "I think we all remember what happened the last time we fought. Can you see me now?"

Jonas growled and tried to push past Oskar. His eyes had fully recovered from whatever Rafe had thrown at him last year, but just the memory of that shit hurt. Months of built-up frustration were about to be released all at once. They'd accepted Rafe because Noah asked them to, but there was only so much a man could take. Even if he died in the attempt, it might be worth it to wipe the smug smile off that asshole's face temporarily.

"Okay, settle down children. The real enemy is out there." Noah appeared from somewhere, and a huge hand landed on Jonas's chest, keeping him immobile. He leaned closer to whisper in Jonas's ear. "Take a break. Calm down. I've got this."

Jonas clenched his teeth before turning and stalking down the hall. He trusted Noah a hell of a lot. They'd walked through fire together, literally, and there was no one else he'd rather have covering his back. But Noah had sure as hell better handle it.

Because if he didn't, Jonas would.

———

It was a wonder JJ didn't trip and fall as she ran blindly down the hallway. She was so angry she could barely see straight but also awash with a raging flush of embarrassment.

She burst through the door to her room, kicking it shut behind her.

"Ugh! I just…" Not sure what to do with the rage, she turned in circles before finally running and diving onto the bed. Her scream was muffled by the pillow.

It still wasn't enough so she rolled and wrapped the bed linens around her. She couldn't see anything or hear anything right now because if it was any of those guys' stupid faces, she was seriously going to punch someone.

There was a quiet knock and then a minute later, another one. JJ figured if she ignored the world long enough, everyone would go away.

She heard the door open and then shut quietly. JJ sighed softly, her warm breath pooling beneath the comforter, thick and stifling. It was tempting to stay under the covers all day but knowing Jonas, he'd snatch the covers off anyway. He liked to face things head on.

Normally that was something she liked also. It was a bit of rub to discover that she could hide her head in the sand with the best of them. But after everything that had happened, her sensitive underbelly was exposed, and she was getting a little tired of taking hits.

"You might as well stop hiding. It's just me."

Surprised at the sound of Lucia's voice, JJ whipped the covers back. Lucia was holding a plate of pancakes and a mug.

"If that's coffee, I'll promise you my firstborn."

Her friend's easy laughter comforted her and drawn to the warmth, JJ finally sat up. She accepted the plate and then moved until her back hit the headboard. The first mouthful of steaming hot pancake drizzled with butter made her moan.

"Okay, I forgive you."

Lucia's gray eyes rounded. "Forgive me? For what?"

"For having such an asshole for a brother," JJ grumbled.

"Well, that part isn't my fault. Nonna always said he was exactly like my dad. So I guess he's to blame."

At the thought of Lucia's deceased parents, JJ instantly felt ashamed. "Sorry. I guess Rafe isn't the only one who doesn't think before speaking."

"It's fine. He was completely out of line. I yelled at him, but I can go yell some more if it makes you feel better."

After a few more mouthfuls of pancake and several bracing sips of coffee, JJ finally felt human.

"I appreciate you coming to check on me and bringing food."

"Of course." Lucia winked. "What are best friends for? I wasn't going to let you suffer back here alone. I wouldn't have stuck around to take shit from the guys either."

"Jonas had me half convinced that no one heard us. That everyone was asleep."

"Um... nobody got any sleep last night, I'm sure." Lucia covered her mouth but JJ could still see her shoulders shaking. "That man of yours sure likes to put on a show."

JJ rolled her eyes. "He's just marking his territory. It couldn't be any more blatant if he'd raised his leg and peed on me."

Lucia was laughing so hard tears pooled in her eyes. "Now that's a visual. The two of you are perfect for each other."

JJ squeezed her eyes closed. "It's just so embarrassing."

Lucia immediately stopped laughing and moved closer.

"Oh honey, no. I know the guys were teasing, but it's all in good fun. You know that, right?"

"I was talking about the whole thing with... Rafe."

JJ kept her eyes closed. It was way too weird to be talking about her former crush on Lucia's brother. But her eyes popped open at Lucia's soft chuckle.

"Seriously, JJ? You thought I didn't know? I'm your *best friend,* and you think I couldn't tell how you felt?"

In hindsight, it was a little ridiculous to think that she'd been so stealthy with her secret. JJ should have known that Lucia would pick up on her crush. After all, no one knew her better. Not even her own mother, who had tried hard to relate to JJ but could never quite understand her brash, aggressive daughter. Her mom was very reserved and soft spoken. Her father had been too busy working to spend much time with her. JJ had spent her teenage years sure her parents would have been much happier with a more docile, sweet type of daughter.

It was only at Lucia's house that she'd felt accepted.

"You always were the only person who really 'got' me."

Lucia glanced at her from the corner of her eye. "But not anymore. Because of Jonas?"

After a brief pause, JJ admitted in a soft voice, "Yeah. Because of Jonas." It felt like a risk even saying it aloud, as if stating it would tempt fate to take it away.

"But now I wonder if being so isolated has caused some of this. Maybe if I'd trusted you more, I would have told you about David before this. Stupid pride might have put Izzy in danger. Because if I'd talked about all this earlier, the guys would have known about David and would have been prepared when he walked in. If they'd known what he was capable of, they never would have let this happen."

Lucia patted her leg. "You can't blame yourself. It probably wouldn't have even mattered. David or Chamaeleon or whatever his name is, knows how to hide. He's ORUS. These guys are trained in how to hide."

Curious, JJ narrowed her eyes. "How do you know all that?"

"Noah probably wasn't supposed to tell me any of that but it's lonely for them, having no one to confide in. But that's part of how ORUS turns them into weapons. They strip them of everything that makes them human. Relationships, friendships, ability to show emotion. These guys are trained to become a blank slate that the government or whoever can use as weapons. When they're in, no one knows who they really are or anything about them. It's like they don't exist."

JJ thought back to all those nights when David had talked to her. He hadn't behaved anything like Lucia described. In fact, she'd gotten the sense that he was hungry to tell her about himself. It wasn't unusual for him to describe his childhood, his friends and the things he wanted for the future, right down to the furniture he planned to build for the dream home he wanted to buy for her.

She sat up suddenly. "It's like they don't exist? But he existed with me. He loved to talk to me."

Lucia looked thoughtful. "For someone like him, with no family or friends, I could see how appealing it would be to have someone to confide in. Maybe he thought it was safe because you were so young and had no idea who he really was?"

The more JJ thought about it, the more it made sense. David definitely hadn't been holding back with her. Even though she'd been young, even at the time she'd been aware that his obsession with her wasn't natural. His happiness had seemed to hinge on impressing her and having her see him as the best and the strongest. Nothing could enrage him faster than any hint she might prefer someone else.

Especially Rafe.

"I think he really was telling me the truth about himself. Stuff that he never thought anyone would find out about, which means he's not as hidden as he thinks. Because we already have everything we need to find him."

JJ turned to Lucia with a triumphant smile. "Me."

CHAPTER ELEVEN

If that stupid asshole didn't wipe that smirk off his face, Jonas was going to wipe it off for him.

Several seats away, Rafe lounged back in one of the conference chairs mirroring Jonas's stance. They glared at each other over Ryan, Dylan, and Noah. Matthias sat closer to the window in front of the monitors. Jonas was pretty sure Noah had arranged the seating this way on purpose so that the two of them couldn't go at it again.

A part of him knew he was being irrational. Any kind of feelings JJ might have had for Rafe were over. *Done. Finito.* She was in love with Jonas. And he was in love with her.

Still, the idea that she'd ever wanted that muscle bound

asshole at any point in her life made Jonas's skin itch. It made him twitchy as fuck and infused him with the desire to hit something. Namely that jackass's face. That sensation wasn't eased any by the smug grin Rafe flashed every time he looked at him. Jonas could practically hear the asshole taunting him. *Oh yeah, she wanted all of this.*

Let it go. It's not important.

The real enemy was out there. The asshole who'd actually tried to hurt JJ. But that was all easier said than done. The whole situation made him want to leave the conference room, drag JJ back to her bedroom, and make her scream his name again, over and over and over.

That can be arranged. And it could be. But then his insecurity would be showing. And he was not going to be insecure about that asshole.

Yeah, he was still smarting from the fight a little over a year ago. The one where Rafe had almost blinded him, and nearly killed both Matthias and Oskar. They'd all lived to tell the tale, and now Rafe was part of the fold. All one big happy family. *Except they weren't.* Well sort of. But Rafe was still an outlier, and Jonas didn't trust him.

Yeah, you do. Because when it comes to his sister, the guy would give his life. Almost did. The real question was if that courtesy extended to the rest of them. Rafe had been more than willing to kill them a year ago.

Jonas forced himself to roll his shoulders and relax. Rafe caught the movement and his brow lifted as a smile teased his lips.

In response, Jonas's hands curled into fists.

Noah slanted the two of them a glance. "Are you two fucking focused? Rafe, sit the fuck up. And Jonas, either quit pouting or go get your girlfriend and go screw her somewhere other than here. You guys work out your shit on your own time then come back when you feel more up to it."

Fuck. Had Noah just scolded his ass? *Didn't you deserve it?* Shit, deserved or not, he didn't fucking like it. But Noah had a point. Rafe might be a supreme asshole but they had bigger fish to fry, and he was letting his personal shit get in the way of things. "I'll take you up on that later. Right now we have work."

"I'm glad you agree with me." Noah rolled his eyes and turned his attention back to the team. "Okay, so like I was saying, from the information that Ian gave us, these are his likely locations. Personally I like this one. It's a mission he's most likely to accept. Lots of exits. Never locked in. As far as we know, as far as Ian has told us, he hasn't checked in. I think —" the conference room doors opened, and all the men lifted their heads to find JJ and Lucia strolling in.

Jonas's gaze pinned to his woman immediately, his eyes raking over her, and he couldn't help but think about everything he'd done to her last night. All the ways he'd made her scream. All the ways he'd made her scream his name. *She's yours. Just get over it already.* He needed to, but the shit was eating at him. When her gaze met his, all her skin turned pink. And it made him want to smile. Yes, she maybe was a little embarrassed, but she hadn't been worried about a damn thing last night. Maybe he'd take Noah up on the idea of taking her to a hotel. She could scream all she wanted there without any embarrassment whatsoever.

He shook his head to clear his mind, and the image of her spread out over a hotel bed with his mouth planted on her pussy took over. *Because now is not the time.* And he was going to have a helluva time explaining to the guys why the hell he wouldn't be able to stand up after this damn meeting.

Noah frowned. "JJ? Sweetheart? What are you two doing here?"

JJ shifted on her feet when Lucia spoke. "JJ has something she thinks might help."

Jonas had never seen JJ shy, or quiet, or modest, or unsure of herself at all. That worried him. Yeah, she was vulnerable with him. But the fact she was displaying it now meant this had something to do with David... with Chamaeleon. And whatever it was, it was part and parcel of everything that had scared her in her life.

"So, Lucia and I were just trying to run through any information that I might have on him. Where he might go, anyone he might call. I think it's safe to say that anyone I might've met when we were together," she said, her gaze away from him when she said the word 'together,' "Was probably a front; fake names, business associates. I will never know who they really were. But the one thing he was really obsessed about was family. He kept talking about us, you know, getting married one day and having kids and moving to a split level home in Bliss, Connecticut. And not just like pie-in-the-sky, oh-one-day kind of dreams. I mean he would pull up houses on real estate websites and pick out specific homes. I don't know, but maybe after all this time he would've finally found a house like that. So maybe if Matthias did a search on homes that were owned by someone with an identity that couldn't be traced back more than the last couple of years, maybe we could find him that way."

Noah nodded. "JJ, that's good. But while he might have bought a house in the last two years, all his activity suggests that he's been here in the city all this time. You're here. You're the object of his obsession. Yeah, he might have wanted to take you to a house or something then, but now it doesn't make sense. He doesn't have you. That idea of happy families and all that shit doesn't apply. You're with someone else."

Jonas grinned at that. And she flushed again. *That's right. You're all mine.*

"I... I know. I just mean when I say he's obsessed, I mean like really obsessed. He wanted everything he thought Rafe had. And I'm telling you, this means something. I can't even believe I didn't think about it until now."

Matthias nodded. "It won't hurt to have a look. Could take a minute though."

She nodded. "Yeah. Okay. I just wanted to make sure I let you guys know."

He hated that sound in her voice. The one where she sounded so defeated. Luckily, she had Lucia in her corner.

"No, JJ. Don't move." Lucia pinned her gaze on Noah. "You guys aren't taking this seriously. JJ's brought you valuable intel. As obsessive as this guy was with her, with the idea of them moving off and living in *our* old neighborhood, Rafe, that's a big fucking deal. You guys need to take this seriously."

Both Rafe and Noah shifted uncomfortably.

Yeah, Lucia had that effect on the two of them. Funny thing was that take-no-prisoners look that JJ usually had them all by the balls with, Lucia was pretty damn good at it when she wanted something, too.

"Matthias, you're going to look into it now. Today. You guys can play, you know, secret government kill squad, all you want. But at the very least, look into this. It took JJ a lot of guts to walk in here."

JJ's gaze met his, and Jonas winked at her. She tucked her chin up and inhaled a deep breath. "Yeah, cool, when I was a teenager I had a crush on Rafe. No big deal. And caveman over here thought it would be a real good idea to brand me last night. Which you all heard, so fair enough.

It's not like this entire office hasn't seen Noah and Lucia going at it, which by the way, *eww* you guys. Seriously, keep it behind closed doors."

Noah just grinned and had a self-satisfied smile on his face.

JJ continued. "The sooner we all get past this, the better for everyone. Look, I know it's not the current plan, foregoing the Ian and kill squad idea, or whatever the fuck that is. But, it's worth looking into. And I'm not leaving the room without your word that you're going to look into it."

From the foot of the table, Matthias nodded. "I've already got a search running."

She nodded. "Well, in that case, I'm going, gentlemen."

Lucia paused giving each of them a stern face. "If a single one of you brings up yesterday to her, I'll kill you myself. And this one," she pointed at Noah, "Won't be able to save you." Then she stormed out after her friend.

Jonas wondered if that applied to him, too. But at this point, he knew better than to fuck with Lucia. All he wanted was Jessica back. The feisty version of her, who didn't take shit from anyone. He wanted to catch this asshole so that she could finally move on with her life and see that she had someone who loved her right in front of her. Someone she would never have to be afraid of.

When JJ and Lucia left the room, Jonas slid a glance over at Noah who shook his head. "Well then. Matthias make sure you get that information to everyone immediately if anything pops. In the meantime, we keep with our current plan. Find any hiding holes he's got. And that takes all men on this team. No matter our differences, right?"

Jonas might not like Rafe, and maybe one day they would eventually bury their hatchet, but for JJ, he would do anything. Anything to see that smile on her face again. So he nodded slowly. "You'll get no problems and no arguments from me."

Noah nodded at him and turned his gaze to Rafe. "What about you, big brother? You gonna keep poking at my boy?"

Rafe tossed his hands up. "As long as he doesn't poke at me, we're good."

Jonas rolled his eyes. That was about as close to a truce as they were going to get. *For now.*

First, they had a chameleon to find.

———

"See, that's the key. I told you there was nothing to be embarrassed about."

JJ stared at Lucia, her mouth open. "Are you kidding me right now? I mean, I'm not shy, but every single one of those guys pretty much heard Jonas um—"

Lucia grinned. "Staking his claim?" She offered helpfully.

"Yes. Staking his claim. It's humiliating."

Lucia put her hand on her head. "Humiliating how? You don't want anyone to know about you and Jonas?"

JJ wrinkled her nose. "Don't be ridiculous. I don't care who knows. I want to shout it from the rooftops."

"Okay, so you shouted it from your bed. What's the problem?"

"I don't know. It was more about how that whole thing unfolded. I mean, it's *embarrassing,* okay? This is me, love-em-and-leave-em JJ. I had a stupid crush, and made a bad decision about a man, and the next thing I know, everyone is all up in my business."

Lucia sighed. "Honey, you have been my best friend since we were kids and we met in Mr. Patterson's class. You think I don't know that you're mostly bravado and hard exterior with a soft, warm, gooey center? What's crazy is you thinking *they* don't know that about you."

JJ scowled. "I'm tough."

Her best friend shook her head. "No one is disputing that, honey. But most of us see that show for what it is, a suit you put on every day. One that keeps you protected. One that keeps you *safe*. And as your best friend, I personally like the suit. I think it's fun. And I know that you need it. You need it to protect the woman that you are. So it's fine. But guess what, we all love the woman inside. The one who's warm, and sweet. The one who buys Earl Grey tea for Matthias just to give him a taste of home. And you know he doesn't drink coffee. You're the one who on her way home buys those German cakes for Oskar and leaves them on his desk. And you never ever say that it's you, but we all know. It's like how you remember Noah's birthday and always try to get him something appropriate. You used to do that for Rafe too when we were kids, remember? You'd always get him some silly little gift. And you've always been there for me. You listened to me when my parents were gone, when Rafe was gone. You are always a rock, and you're always the one guaranteed to make me laugh. To let me see that there is a fun side to life. So, we all love you and we see the real you. We love the sass, we love the mouth. It's part of the fun. But there's also the you underneath it all that we see and love. So you know what? No one cares about how you had a crush on Rafe. It's not like we didn't know, I told you that already. Rafe knew. Noah knew. *Everyone* knew. So what if the rest of the guys know?"

JJ sighed. "It's just, ugh, I don't like being vulnerable."

Lucia grinned. "No one does, that's why it's called being vulnerable."

Her goddaughter took that opportunity to wake up from her nap and screeched the house down. Isabella was never a fan of waking up alone. "I guess the princess summons me. I'll be right back." Lucia ran to get the baby, who likely needed to be changed or fed, or a combination of both.

JJ went into the kitchen and pulled the fridge open, determined to go for the red velvet cake in the back that Noah had brought from Nonna's. When she pulled out the cake, she almost jumped a mile and splattered cake all over her face when she found Rafe leaning against the doorway.

"'Sup, JJ?"

Her face went hot. And no doubt she was bright crimson at this point. *Fantastic.* "Hey Rafe. Want a slice?"

He shook his head. "But if you have a spare fork, I'll take a bite."

JJ pulled open the cutlery drawer and pulled out two forks. She handed one over to him, before digging her own into the cake and shoving a fat piece of delicious goodness into her mouth. Oh God. Yes. Sugar and icing were just the balm her bruised ego needed.

Rafe took a bite and actually moaned. "Jesus Christ. That's one thing I missed, you know? Nonna's cooking. And her baking. Pretty much everything actually."

JJ sighed. "You know, we never even talked about it, you and I. What it must have been like for you. I mean I'm the best friend, so I guess I've always been on the outside looking in at that whole situation."

Rafe shook his head. "We didn't see you that way. You were part of the family. Yeah, at the time sometimes I thought you were my sister's annoying best friend. But you were a fixture in Nonna's house. You were one of the people I missed."

"Yeah, I guess everyone's heard how I missed you, so there's that."

He chuckled low. "You really think I didn't know?"

"Shit, I guess I wasn't real subtle."

He nodded. "Pretty much. I mean you used to stare at me a lot. And admittedly, I caught you and Lucia practicing kissing on your hands once. You referred to your hand as Rafe. That was a pretty clear sign."

JJ covered her face with her hands. "Oh. My. God. That's almost worse than last night."

He grinned. "Yeah. Don't worry about it. I thought it was cute. Besides, have you seen me? I'm pretty hot."

She snorted. "I was 13. Cut me some slack."

His chuckle was low and deep. "I'll cut you some slack when you cut yourself some. It's no big deal, JJ." He cleared his throat "I—I do owe you an apology though."

She took another forkful of cake. "For what?"

"For never saying I'm sorry to you. Like I said, you were like family to me. My annoying-little-sister kind of family, but family nonetheless, and I never said I was sorry for the years of pain you went through as a result of my decision."

JJ forced herself to swallow the piece of cake around the sudden onset of sawdust in her mouth. "You don't owe me an apology. I made my decision about David on my own. That had nothing to do with you."

"I don't know. I feel a little responsible. If I'd been there, I would've steered you away from him. I would've seen him for what he was. It was my job to protect you."

"Stop. It wasn't your job to protect me. *I* made a bad choice. And I suffered the consequences. The good news is, now I won't make choices like that anymore."

He nodded. "All the same though. I'd personally like to kick that guy's ass for you. You were a good kid, and I did love you. I *do* love you. Not the way that Jonas does. And I'm pretty sure he's probably going to want to kill me for saying it."

JJ giggled. "Yeah. He's still kinda mad at you for everything that happened last year."

Rafe rolled his eyes. "You try to kill a guy *one* time. I swear, it was a misunderstanding."

She grinned. "That was one hell of a misunderstanding.

Are you guys ever going to tell me who exactly it is that you work for or what you do, or did, or whatever?"

He studied her for a moment his expression impassive. "Lucia told you?"

"Not much. I sort of guessed that you guys were more than just a security company, but she hasn't really said explicitly. So I let my imagination run wild. And my imagination is very, very good."

He nodded. "Well, yeah, I guess we don't exactly keep a lot of things super-secret."

"So this isn't the part where you tell me now that I know that you have to kill me?"

"Nope. Right now my job is to protect you. You, Lucia, Nonna, Noah, and by extension these idiots." He shrugged. "You're all family. That's how it goes. For what it's worth, that was good intel that you brought into the conference room. I know it can't have been easy to walk in there after — after last night."

She shrugged. "Well, talking to Lucia helped me remember his level of obsession. You know what's funny? I didn't even realize it then, but I probably fed into his obsession. Every time I would talk to him about how much I missed you or how much it hurt Lucia not having you there, he would ask me to talk about you and told me it was therapy, that it would help me feel better. And like an idiot, I played into that."

Rafe took another bite. "You're not an idiot. You trusted the wrong guy, yes, but you did nothing wrong there. You were being open and kind and trying to move on with your life after the bullshit I put you guys through."

"Yeah, still feels like I should've seen something. But he was everything I thought I wanted, you know? Like the perfect kind of guy. And then I saw it was something much more dangerous, something darker than that. I didn't understand it. Now I see how much he hated you. I mean he was obsessed with me, but only because I had a crush on you. You were the real one, the one he wanted to hurt. I didn't see that until now."

"Well, the good news is he's not gonna get the chance. We're going after him before he even comes anywhere near us. You're safe now."

For the first time in her life, she actually believed that. Between Jonas, Noah, Rafe, and everyone else, she knew that she was safe here. Safer than anywhere else in the world.

"You know, I've been thinking about what I just said. He *is* obsessed with me. But not as much as he's obsessed with you. A part of me feels like the only reason he was ever so fixated on me was because of you in the first place. I keep thinking if I make myself bait or something, that would bring him running, but I don't think so anymore. I think *you're* the one he wants. I think he'd do anything to get a shot at you."

Rafe stood straight. And then he studied her for a long moment. "You know, JJ, you might be absolutely right about that."

CHAPTER TWELVE

"You still got your panties in a twist, or are you ready to work?" Rafe's voice was low as they sat in the dark under cover of bushes.

Jonas slid him a glance as they waited for the signal from Matthias and Noah. Moonlight was the only light they had to go by, and if push came to shove, they had their night-vision goggles ready to go. They'd been sitting there for fifteen minutes in tense silence. Neither one of them wanting to give way.

"My panties aren't in a twist. It would be a shame to do that to Italian silk."

Rafe chuckled. "Fair enough."

"Since we're here and all, I guess now's a good time to ask if you're sure about this," Jonas mumbled.

Rafe's jaw tensed. But when he spoke, his voice was flat. "Yes. Besides, no one's supposed to get hurt today. I'm only *playing* assassin again. It's not for real."

"You know, you, Noah, and Matthias all get that same look on your face whenever you talk about what you used to do."

Rafe narrowed his gaze and did another sweep through his binoculars. "Yeah. ORUS changed every single one of us. That's the problem when you do that kind of job when you still have a soul. There are plenty of guys in there who have no soul." He shrugged. "Who knows, maybe now it's the kind of organization it was supposed to be in the first place. Only taking out the worst of the worst, cleaning up the trash. But, I still don't trust them. It's hard to say."

"You regret bringing Noah in?"

Rafe didn't even look at him as he answered. "Every fucking day. I mean it wasn't like I brought him in myself you know. That was Ian. The kid saved Ian's life so that was that. Ian thought he was saving him. The problem was Ian didn't see the toll it was taking. And I had to train him, or he'd get killed. So I regret him being in that life, but I'm glad I taught him to be the best he could be. It kept him alive. And you can't get out if you're dead, right?"

Jonas nodded. "Yeah, that's one way of looking at it."

After a long moment, Rafe asked, "So, we cool on the JJ thing?"

Jonas clenched his jaw. "Yeah. We're fine. As long as you get that she's mine."

Rafe chuckled. "Man, what the fuck is it with you guys when you fall in love? All caveman and shit. Me Tarzan, she Jane. I swear you and Noah are ridiculous. I mean, you're too pretty to be a caveman anyway. You're too Metro."

Jonas shook his head. "There is nothing wrong with a little manscaping and decent clothes. You might try something other than basic black all the time."

Rafe frowned. "What's wrong with black? It goes with everything. And helps, you know, when you're trying to kill people. They can't see you coming."

Jonas had to hold back a chuckle. "Seriously? I'm beginning to doubt your sanity."

"What? I'm just being honest."

"All I'm saying is it wouldn't hurt you to put a little effort into it. You know mix it up, change your fabrics."

"Look, I'm just going to leave the pretty-boy antics to you and Noah."

"Oskar sees nothing wrong with a little blazer every now and again."

"Yeah, you realize you're talking about the accountant, right?"

Jonas considered that. "Yeah, you have a point there."

They'd sat in relative silence for several more minutes when Rafe frowned and grumbled. "Something's wrong."

Jonas shifted in his position slightly. His fucking arm was falling asleep in his current position. "Why do you say that?"

Rafe shook his head. "It's quiet. Almost *too* quiet. We haven't had a single person walking a dog or turning off their porch lights. It's like the whole neighborhood's dead."

Jonas frowned. "Please don't say the word dead."

Rafe pressed his comm unit. "Matthias, can you verify we have movement in the house? And while you're at it check the other two neighboring houses. The street's too quiet."

Matthias's voice came back in the comm unit. "I still see heat sigs. There's a body upstairs, master bedroom. So target is there. Still alive as far as I can tell. Other houses, everyone's snug in bed."

It was funny, as soon as Rafe had said it, Jonas started to get that all-too-familiar feeling that something was wrong. Something was *very* wrong. He couldn't put his finger on it though. He pressed his own comm unit. "And we're sure this is the location Ian identified? Because Rafe's right. Something's not right here. Even my gut's saying it. And I'm not some superspy."

Next to him, Rafe chuckled. "You'll do okay. I mean cop senses aren't as good as spy senses, but they're not bad."

Jonas rolled his eyes. "I'm serious. Something is wrong. We've been out here for an hour and a half. Either he's a no-show or he found another way in that house that we don't know about."

Noah's voice was crisp. "Roger. Alpha unit, move into the house. Secure the target if you have too. But you're right, something's off. Beta team, fall back to their flanks and watch their six."

Despite their stiff bodies from lying in position for so long under the hedges of the house across the street, the house that had been in foreclosure for over six months, Jonas and Rafe sprang into action, darting quickly across the street and ducking for cover. At this point, everyone was silent. He and Rafe communicated with a series of sign language and hand gestures as they approached the side door of the house. When they entered, all was quiet in the garage, but there was an eerie silence that fell over them like an icy cold blanket. In seconds, Rafe had the deadbolt off, and then Jonas flipped the security alarm.

The moment they stepped in the house though, they knew something was wrong.

Jonas's voice was tight as he spoke into the comm unit. "Matthias. We have a problem. The house, it's too cold in here."

Noah's voice was harsh. "Get to the target now."

Gun drawn, Jonas followed quickly behind Rafe, both of them clearing each room in succession. When they reached the master bedroom, Rafe went first and Jonas watched his back. Gun aimed, at the ready. And then from behind him, he heard it, Rafe's rather inventive cursing. When he spoke into his comm unit, the anger dripped and vibrated from every single word. "We have a fucking problem. Target's goddamn dead."

Matthias's voice came through loud and clear. "Fuck a twat. What the fuck do you mean he's dead, mate?"

"I'm talking ashes to ashes. Time to baste the formaldehyde turkey."

"That's not fucking possible. I'm showing your heat signatures and his."

Jonas glanced over his shoulder. Rafe was right. The guy was too still in the bed. Not moving. "Yeah, Rafe's not lying. The guy's not moving."

Matthias cursed on the other line. "Then why do I see a fucking heat signature?"

Rafe sighed. "The son-of-a-bitch used a warming blanket. Temperature's currently set to one hundred degrees. And he's tucked in tight, like a cocoon. Hate to say it, but he's fucking cooking in here."

On the other end of the line, Noah swore. "Fucking Ian. We've been played."

———

Jonas and Rafe carried the body out of the house into the back yard where they at least had some cover. Noah and Matthias met with them within a minute.

"The people in the houses next door, they're all dead." Noah muttered. "*No one* was supposed to die."

Jonas stared at him. "We're not dealing with someone sane are we? He not only took out our target, he took out innocent civilians."

"Jonas, you think I don't know that? You think I don't feel the pressure?"

Rafe stepped between the two of them. "Never thought that I'd be doing this, but we need to focus. We need to identify the people in the houses next door, identify the target for confirmation, and get the fuck out."

In their comm units, the alarm sound blared. Rafe glanced at Matthias. "What is that?"

"Proximity alarms. We have incoming."

Rafe and Jonas immediately put on their night-vision goggles.

"I've got three guys coming from the south."

Rafe drew his gun. "I see two coming from the east.

Matthias and Noah went on red alert. What they didn't account for, was the basement door bursting open, and two men running out.

All four of them backed up against each other to face their opponents. Their guns had silencers, and they each had extra ammo. But this was not the kind of fight they wanted. None of this was supposed to happen. *You're a cop.* Ex-cop.

In situations like this, he'd call for fucking backup. *Well your backup's here. Do what you gotta do.* Jonas knew that some people were going to end up dead. He just prayed it was none of his team. He turned toward the two guys that had barged out of the basement, Rafe chuckled before sheathing his gun back in his holster. "What the fuck are you doing, Rafe?"

The guy must have completely lost it because he laughed. "It's time to have some fun."

A swift glance around told Jonas that Matthias had also put away his gun. Instead, he had out knives. *Knives at a goddamn gunfight.* He knew what happened to people who carried knives. They fucking got shot.

Noah was the only one who was acting sane. He at least had out his gun, scratch that, two. Okay then, so it was like that.

In the span of a second, Jonas wasn't paying attention to what was happening with his friends. He was fighting for his life. He squeezed off a bullet, hitting one of the guys in the upper thigh, but the asshole didn't even go down. Instead he just kept on coming. "What the fuck?"

Somewhere near his right, Rafe called out, "Body Armor. That's why the guns are useless unless you can fire a kill shot at a moving target."

Well fuck him. Before he knew what was happening the shorter guy on the right lunged at him and knocked him over. The air whooshed out of his lungs as the asshole pressed all his weight on top of him.

From beneath, Jonas defended against the blows. The taller slimmer one on the left had jumped onto Noah.

Noah had fired a kill shot for one of the guys coming from the south, but the other was still coming. And now he had more company. Jonas had to get the fuck up off the ground. Somewhere above his head to the left, he heard the slicing of knives, metal on metal, and a series of grunts, kicks, and curses.

All Jonas could do was block the blows and try to survive. But then the guy on him made one fatal mistake. He eased back, to reach for a weapon maybe? But he didn't know that Jonas had Jujutsu training.

Jonas loved nothing more than to grapple if he could get a leg in. He wedged his knee between his body and the guy's chest then shoved back. The guy flew backwards, and Jonas was on his feet in a second.

Then it was a matter of hand to hand. The good news was this guy was not as good as Rafe. Oh he had been trained. Really, really fucking well-trained. Like assassin trained.

Jonas took a left cross to the jaw and staggered. Then the guy moved forward, grabbing him by the shoulders and delivering a series of knees. *Motherfucker*. The pain spread through his chest as his ribs took a pounding. But on the last knee kick, Jonas grabbed him under the thigh, and unsettled him enough to knock him on his back.

And then it was on. Jonas pounced on him, raining blows on his face. The guy reached underneath him, and Jonas heard the *shhhht* sound of metal being unsheathed. *A knife.*

He leaned back in the nick of time to avoid a slice of the knife across his jugular, but the damn thing caught his arm. *Son of a bitch.*

Jonas grabbed the guy's hand and dropped several elbows on his face. But even though the guy's eye was glued shut now with blood, he still tried to work his legs out from under Jonas.

Jonas pinned one of his arms with a knee, which essentially put his dick right in the guy's face. "Hey man, maybe you like balls in the face, but now would be a good fucking time to stop moving."

The asshole beneath him still tried to come at him with a knife, raising his arm, and Jonas had to duck and weave and grapple for that free arm. When he grabbed it, it was a battle of wills and a battle of strength. The guy tried to turn the knife around on him, but Jonas didn't let go. No, then it would be lights out. Party over. And then what the fuck would happen to JJ?

JJ. Fuck. Just thinking about her gave him the extra boost of strength he needed. And with all his might, he turned the guy's wrist, shoving the knife down into his neck. It took several seconds, but eventually he stopped moving.

Don't stay still. On your feet. There's more of them than there are of you guys. When he turned, Jonas found that one of the guys that had come from the south was already dead. Another one was down. One guy was limping and reaching for his gun. Jonas went right for him. He was running, stepping on his hand before bending down, grabbing the gun, and twisting his hand until he heard it crack.

The guy made a muffled moan, but tried to twist around and grab Jonas's ankle. "Stop fucking with me or I will kill you." But he still reached for the weapon.

What the hell was wrong with these guys? None of them seemed to want to live. Jonas had no choice. One shot to the head. Without even thinking about it he dropped the guys arm and turned to face his friends.

Matthias had one down on the ground, they were wrestling with one of the knives, but then Matthias head butted him and made sure that knife sliced home and implanted in his neck. Then the kid was up on his feet in no time. His face was covered in blood, and his hands were up, both knives gripped by their handles, ready to slice and fight.

Noah delivered a kick to the skull of the guy he had been fighting with. But the guy refused to go down. He came at Noah with fists and knees, but Noah dodged and avoided them all. He delivered a couple of good knee strikes before a very nice elbow to left hook combination. The guy staggered back and delivered his own elbow, ringing Noah's bell. Before Noah could rebound, there was a *pffft* sound and the guy sagged to the ground. Noah whirled around, hands up. Rafe just shrugged.

"You were playing with your food. You want a work out, I'll give you one."

Noah nodded. "Thanks. Fucking lost my gun."

Jonas handed a gun to him. "This it?"

"Yeah. Those assholes had me pinned down and took it off me."

Rafe give him a wry grin. "Not the first time I saved you in a firefight."

Noah clocked him on the arm. "Probably not the last." Then he checked in on each of the rest of them. "Kid? You good?"

Matthias, who still had knives at the ready and was breathing hard and heavy standing over the carcass of the man he'd carved up, didn't respond at first.

Under normal circumstances, Jonas would have said the kid was a good kid. Loved his nerdy T-shirts, and the superhero movies. Given the way some of the female clients smiled at him shyly, women didn't think he was too hard on the eyes. And there was a somewhat innocent quality about him. Women tended to want to take care of him. Hell, they all looked at him as some kind of little brother. But at that moment, with his knives in his hands and pure, visceral hate and anger radiating over his body and his face, Jonas knew the truth. Matthias was all killer. This was who he was underneath the carefully crafted exterior. Peel back one layer of the onion, and it was clear the kid was no one to fuck with.

Matthias nodded. "Yep, fine mate."

Noah's voice was soothing. Quiet almost. "Good. Then why don't you go ahead and put your knives away, and step back. Head back to the communications van. Call our cleanup crew. I want IDs on all these guys. Preferably before we head over to deal with Ian."

Fuck, they weren't done. "You think he sent them?" Jonas asked.

"Not sure. But he knew exactly where we would be tonight, which means either he told someone, or we were set up. Either way, he's gonna have to answer some questions about it."

Rafe went over to Matthias. He didn't touch him though. "Kid, did you hear Noah? He needs you to get the ball rolling. The time for killing is done. Back away."

Matthias just blinked back him. There was a gleam in his eyes, like he wanted to go toe to toe with Rafe. Like he was desperate for a rematch of what had gone down a little over a year ago. Rafe adjusted his footing so he was on the balls of his feet, hands up in what looked like a defensive posture, but Jonas recognized it as the fight stance for krav maga. "Matthias. Stand down."

Noah's voice took an edge as well. "Kid, comms. Call in Delaney."

That seemed to shake him out of it. And he blinked several times. When he saw the position of his knives, he sheathed them and met Rafe's gaze. "Sorry." When he turned, he nodded at Noah. "I'm good."

Noah visibly relaxed. "Yeah, I know. Get on, we'll bring all the bodies out. Photograph them, so at least you can have them cataloged. And then it'll make the cleaner's job easier."

As Rafe and Noah headed to the house on the left, Jonas stared after Matthias. Just how dangerous was the kid? He didn't have time to ask those questions though, because they needed to clean up and then find out if Ian had set them the fuck up.

CHAPTER THIRTEEN

Jonas still couldn't believe that Noah was letting him take point. And, well, he did feel like sort of a badass with his own personal kill squad behind him. When they bypassed Ian's security easily, in through the front door, they found the new leader of ORUS in his kitchen, two guns pointed in their direction and a grenade on his countertop.

"Wow, dramatic aren't you? You can put the guns away. A grenade? Jesus." Jonas slid a glance to Noah. "Is every single one of you a prima donna? We just came to talk." He turned his attention back to Ian, who hadn't lowered his guns at all. The guy's right eye twitched when he saw Rafe and Matthias come in behind him and Noah.

"What do you want?"

Jonas palmed his own weapon. "Look Ian, we're just here to talk. About that little death squad you sent for us?"

"Death squad?"

Jonas nodded as he rounded the counter. "Yeah, the team of seven you sent after us, after you told us that everything was all set and we could set the trap and spring it for your boy Chamaeleon. David. Jesus, do all of you have code-names?"

From behind him, Rafe chuckled. "Yeah. You wish you were cool enough."

Jonas shook his head. "I'll stick with Jonas Castillo if you don't mind. Has a nicer ring to it. So anyway, Chamaeleon left us a few little presents. Dead presents. I swear, your boy's like a rabid fucking dog. He killed the target. *Dead.* He killed innocent civilians in the two neighboring homes."

Ian's brows snapped down as he glared at Noah. "What?"

"Don't look at Noah, look at me. I'm the one who's fucking pissed off. I'm the one who's trying to protect the woman I love. So you're going to start talking, you're going to call off the kill squad that's on its way here to protect you right now, and then we're going to have a conversation about your boy David West."

Ian lowered his guns and carefully picked up the grenade, opened the drawer underneath the counter, and placed it back inside. Then slowly, he pulled the phone out of his back pocket. He tapped in a few numbers, and put it to his ear. Jonas could only assume that someone on the other and had answered when he started speaking. "Code 754312. Orion. Condor has flown." He hung up then. "It wasn't a trap. I didn't set you up."

Noah shrugged. "Ian. You and I go way back. In some ways, I have you to thank for the life that I have. But you need to stop fucking lying. Why are you covering for him?"

"I'm not covering. I did everything as we discussed. I let it slip that we were letting Rafe back in the fold. I simply discussed it with him as we talked about who the target might be. After that, it was up to him to get information. And it looks like he did."

Noah leaned against the countertop. "Yeah, he got there before us. He set up the whole goddamn house. Turned the temperature down, had warming blankets on the guy so that we'd think we had a live body inside. And then, I don't know what kind of armor you guys have now, but he was able to conceal the watchdogs he had in the basement."

Ian sighed. "Temperature in the house very cold?"

Matthias nodded. "Yeah, fucking frigid, mate."

Ian nodded. "We have these new thermo-suits. They serve a dual purpose. Keep your body temperature nice and even, while showing nothing on the exterior. So if you have heat sensors like you guys clearly did, they won't pick it up. And they also act as excellent bulletproofing. Better than Kevlar. Lighter, faster. Recently, we had body disposal for a couple of agents we lost, and their suits came up as unlogged."

Noah threw up his arms. "And you think now is the best time to fucking tell us?"

"How the fuck was I supposed to know? I inherited this goddamn problem; an inheritance by the way, that you perpetrated."

"Like you got the poor end of the deal? Fancy house, more money than you know what to do with, and your own personal kill squad."

Ian shook his head. "You know that's not me. I've never been in this for the power. You know why I do this."

Jonas slid a glance at Noah. "You mean there are reasons to become a homicidal assassin?"

"Can it, Castillo," Rafe muttered.

Jonas turned on Rafe. "Really? We can just roll up in here to your leader and I don't get to ask questions?"

Ian sighed. "Not about my personal life, no. But listen, I know that Chamaeleon is a problem. He was a problem for Orion before me."

Jonas had to take control of the conversation again. If he left it to Noah and Rafe, they'd all be standing around in a circle jerk for another hour. And if he left it to Matthias, every one of them would be dead. Eventually, he and Noah would have to talk about the kid. Because there was something dangerous lurking just underneath the surface with him.

"Okay, look. Start talking, Ian."

"Fine. David West, also known as Chamaeleon, has been an agent since maybe a year before Noah came on board. Brash, uncontrollable, obsessive. Rafe, he looked up to you. He wanted to *be* you, maybe. When you were taken out of play, he became even more obsessed with your life. Started following around your sister, your grandmother, your sister's friend."

Jonas advanced on him, grabbing by the lapels. "You fucking knew?"

With a series of practiced moves, Ian had himself free. But Jonas wasn't going to let up and advanced on him again.

In flash, Rafe had him in a choke hold. "Easy does it, let the man talk." Rafe easily restrained Jonas until he forced himself to relax. Then he was released.

"I didn't personally know. It was only after I went through the employee files that I found the notes. He was obsessed. And that was his MO. There'd been a girl before he became ORUS. He hurt her, killed her. Evidence points to an accident, but still."

"Jesus Christ," Jonas swore.

Ian frowned as he leaned back against the sink. "My predecessor saw skills that could be honed. But, his obsessive personality was a problem. DeMarco, he knew that Orion regarded you as one of his best agents. Considering how young you were and how quickly you rose, he saw you as the one to emulate."

Rafe clenched his jaw. "My record is nothing to be emulated."

Ian narrowed his gaze but made no comment about Rafe and his record. "After you were gone, Orion was worried about the blowback. West was *too* obsessed, wanted to be in every aspect of your life, DeMarco. When Orion found out he wasn't just following but had inserted himself into your family, he was taken out of play and sent on an overseas, long-term mission. Five years. After I became Orion I was doing an assessment on all the agents and discovered he was still active. DeMarco, your personal files are buried. But West must have had access to them after your death. It's possible he knows you even better than Noah does."

"You want to tell me why you didn't take him out?" Noah asked.

"I'm still digging through all the information and cleaning house with my agents. Most of them are true to the cause, patriots. There are some that were either forcibly removed, or let go. I should have done the same with West. But until now, he was an unknown."

Jonas could only stare at him and then back at Noah and Rafe. "So all of you are telling me you had all this information at your fingertips, in essence, and no one did a thing?"

Ian shook his head. "I didn't know. When I brought him back in play to assess him to see if he'd be fit for duty, I had no idea. All I knew was that the work he'd done overseas was solid. I didn't know I'd be triggering his obsession again. We all learned that the hard way. Let me bring him in. I have men at the ready to do it."

Jonas shook his head. "Fuck no. Like we trust your men."

Noah agreed with him. "No. We'll use our guys."

"Look, I want him gone just as much as you do. I've authorized shoot to kill orders on him."

Normally that should've triggered Jonas's old cop genes. But this time it didn't. West had already proven that he was a psychopath. And that he was not above taking a baby, or her nanny, or killing an innocent victim. He had to be put down. Jonas turned his attention back to Ian. "So what's our plan?"

"I've narrowed down a few possible locations. The best places to flush him out."

Jonas nodded. "Fine. Then let's get to work."

"So let me understand, you guys are going to go back out there and search out all of his favorite hiding spots, after he sprang a trap for you and sent men to kill you?"

Jonas cupped his hands over JJ's cheeks and traced his thumb over her bottom lip. "We're going to be fine. I came home to you after the last time, didn't I?"

"Beaten and bloody. You promised me you would be safe."

He did love it when her temper was up. But he didn't want her to worry. "I know. I know what I said. It was unexpected. But we're not going in blind. We'll have ORUS backing us, we'll be fine."

"I don't believe that. You need better backup."

Jonas chuckled bitterly. "There's no such thing. The kind of situations that Noah has gotten people out of... they have connections like you wouldn't believe."

She glanced up at him curiously. "You mentioned that once before, that Noah got you out of trouble but I wasn't sure if I should ask."

"You can ask me anything you want, you know that." He

took a deep breath. "I was in a bad place. There was a woman."

JJ glanced at him from the corner of her eye. "Isn't there always?"

His arm tightened around her waist. "It wasn't like that. Emily needed help. We'd responded to domestic calls there before but she always declined to press charges. Her husband was a wealthy local businessman, lots of friends in high places, so he didn't appreciate some small time cop sticking his nose where it didn't belong."

Her hand caressed the side of his face. "You were trying to help her, weren't you?"

"Yeah. Convinced her to press charges. Then the next thing I knew, I was being arrested for assault. It was my word against his about what happened. I was going to go down for sure, he was friends with the Chief of Police and plenty of judges. Emily was the only one who could testify that I hadn't raised a hand against her but in the end, she sided with her husband. After everything I'd done to try to help her, it wasn't enough. I still don't know how Noah got me out of that one but the next thing I knew, I was being released from jail and told by the chief that my resignation had been accepted. I was too shaken to ask many questions."

JJ pulled him close, resting her head against his chest. It was exactly what he needed right then, the warmth of her embrace permeating the chill thoughts of the past always brought.

"It wasn't your fault, Jonas. You did everything you could. Sometimes, even when you do all you can, it just doesn't work out."

"Exactly," Jonas stated, leaning back so he could look her in the eye. "Which is why I don't want you anywhere near this. Noah has called in help from some friends. Rafe has called in some help from the feds. It'll be okay. And the team, we're together on this."

"Okay, fine, I hear you. But I still think I should come with you. We all know I make really good bait."

Jonas chuckled and tugged her against him. "No. You understand I lost years off my life watching you stroll right up to that asshole and proceed to start screaming at him, right? I can't do it again. I am not strong enough to do that again, so no can do."

JJ shoved at him and he released her. "What's that supposed to mean? I can take care of myself you know."

"Sweetheart, I know. I believe in you. I do. But, all I want to do is keep you safe. You are my heart and my love, and more than once I've had to watch you face complete terror at this guy's hands. I can't do that again. I don't know what I would do if I lost you."

"Well I don't know what I would do if I lost you. I mean, what am I supposed to do without you? I had never planned on falling in love, and now I am. *You* did that to me."

Jonas chuckled. "Well, sweetheart, you're right about that. And if you stop yelling at me, I can do it again."

"Are you serious right now?"

He held up his hands. "Well, it's true, I am irresistible. And I turned my charm on you. So I mean obviously you would fall in love."

She poked him in the chest. "This is not funny. I'm not used to loving someone."

He laughed. "You love people all the time. You just don't want them to know that you love them. Only difference is now I *know*."

"Yeah, but don't go getting all smug about it."

Jonas hugged her tighter. "Me, smug? Never. Now, why don't you help me get out of this battle gear, and you can kiss my boo-boos and admonish me for all the reasons you're mad at me."

"Sex is not going to solve this. I want to help. I want to do *something*. Anything. Let me ride in the van or whatever it is. I can run the communications."

"JJ." She huffed and held her shoulders stiff. "Jessica." The use of her name had her body softening a little bit, and he was willing to use whatever he could to get in her good graces. "Sweetheart, I love you. But I can't let you do this. And if you try, I really will lock you inside this penthouse."

"You are welcome to try. See how well that works out for you. I swear to God you'll be missing a nut in no time."

His lips tipped into smile. "There are more pleasurable things you can do my nuts."

"You keep talking, jackass, and no one's going near your nuts for a very long time."

Jonas grinned. God he loved her sassy mouth. "Yes, I hear you. But, that's really biting off that perfect pussy to spite your own libido. You're not going to cut me off because you need me too much. I bring you all the good orgasms."

She still whacked at him. "So what? I'm sure if I found Lucia's giant toy, it would get the job done too."

"Oh, you wound me." He placed a hand over his chest. "Don't be mad at me. I'm just trying to keep you safe. That's the only thing that matters to me right now and for the rest of my life. Keeping you safe and loving you. Two main directives, that's all I've got."

She harrumphed. "You know, you're not supposed to be so sweet."

"I've always been sweet. You were just too busy sniping at me to notice."

She narrowed those beautiful eyes at him. "Me and you, who was doing the sniping?"

Jonas nipped along her neck. Why did she always smell so good? "I think we know the answer to that."

She groaned and her breath caught. "You. I'm an angel. Ask anyone."

Jonas laughed as he nuzzled her throat. "Yes, maybe an angel of torment. Now come on, I need you to kiss my boo-boos. And I'll sweeten the deal. I'll match you kiss for kiss. Right now I need the woman I love. I need to hold her, need to touch her soft skin, I need her to touch me. What do you say?"

"Well, when you put it like that how could I say no?"

CHAPTER FOURTEEN

She knew what he was trying to do. Distract her. Seduce her with those kisses that always made her forget her own name so she *wouldn't* be thinking about the possibility of him being hurt, or worse, dealing with the nightmare of her past.

"Are you trying to seduce me into dropping this subject?"

He looked her right in the eye. "Yes. Because I don't want you worrying about any of this shit. I'm going to fix it for you."

Even though she knew he was trying to do something good, something positive for her, JJ was done sitting back and letting others be in control. There had been a time she'd wanted that, when she was young and lonely and grieving. But she'd also like to think that she'd learned from her mistakes. Having a man want to control things for her had never ended well.

"You're trying to look out for me, I get it." JJ put her palm gently against his cheek. "But having someone take care of things for me isn't what I want. I've had a man want to take care of everything before. You've seen how that ended up."

Jonas rested his forehead against hers. "I would never treat you like that. My impulse to take care of you doesn't stem from possession. It's just caring. I want to make your life easier and make you happy. Most of all, I want you to be safe."

JJ nodded. She already knew that in her heart, but it helped to hear it stated. Being with David had damaged her confidence in her own judgment and decision making. But sometimes when things in life were shitty, all you could do was grab onto anything good. And this was good. Being with Jonas was explosive and intense but also sweet and comforting. If you'd asked her just a few months ago if she thought this kind of happiness and trust was possible, she would have flat out denied it. *I've become a believer*, she thought as she gazed into his eyes.

His love had made her a believer.

"Kiss me, Jonas. Make me forget all this craziness and all this fear. Let's have one more night where it's just us."

Jonas watched her with knowing eyes then smiled that gentle lilt of his lips that she loved. "It's not going to be just one night, baby. Something this good is meant to be."

Despite his words, he pulled her close and covered her lips with his. JJ could taste the saltiness of her tears mingling with his distinctive flavor but didn't stop. Instead she held him closer. If she'd learned anything over the course of her life, it was that right now was all she had. Each moment was to be savored, and there was so much to taste and touch and hold.

"You're so strong," she whispered. Her cheeks warmed when their eyes met. "I love everything about you."

"Stop. You're going to make me blush."

JJ nuzzled the strong pecs that she loved to rest her head against. His sharp intake of breath when her lips skimmed over his nipple thrilled her. With one hand he reached over his head and yanked his shirt off. Immediately her hands were out, caressing the silken skin and pressing against the hard muscle beneath.

"I love your hair and those big blue eyes. Nothing in the world affects me like seeing those eyes watching me. You make me stand taller, JJ."

Determined not spend any more time worrying, JJ tugged at his belt. The hard length pressing against the front of his jeans was practically pointing at her already. Maybe once she had him in her hand, she could forget all the bad things lurking in the background and just enjoy this precious connection they'd forged together.

"Hey, it's all going to be okay." JJ covered his hand with hers and together they slid the zipper of his jeans down. He stood briefly to push them off, almost tripping as he rushed to remove his boots.

JJ laughed and then followed his lead, their eyes never leaving each other as articles of clothing flew around them, landing in piles on the floor. They came together on the bed in a pile of naked skin, seeking mouths, and greedy hands.

Jonas let out a deep moan when her hands landed on his ass and squeezed.

"Damn, you don't play fair."

She bit his ear. "No, I don't. You know what I want."

He reached over to the nightstand and pulled out a condom. "A guy tries to have some finesse and no one appreciates it."

She helped him put the condom on, pushing it down his length with gentle strokes. "Oh I appreciate all of your finesse."

He clenched his teeth. "You really don't play fair. Your hands feel amazing on me."

Suddenly he turned them so that she was straddling him. Turnabout was fair play, and JJ found herself hovering right over his hard cock, the length brushing against her clit every time she breathed.

"Ride me, baby. Show me how much you want it."

Hearing him ask for it was so arousing. JJ loved how they could say anything to each other.

"That's what you want?" she teased, lowering herself to rock back and forth against him. His hands landed on her hips and JJ gasped as the tip of his cock slipped in.

Teasing him had become her own personal torture. So she decided she'd earned her satisfaction. Placing her hands firmly on his chest, JJ bore down, taking him all the way in. Her muscles clamped down on him immediately, the erotic drag through her tight muscles making her shiver.

"Every time," Jonas gritted out. "You fucking destroy me. Every single time."

JJ panted as she worked her hips, every thrust hitting right in the perfect spot. All the while his hands roamed her skin, making her senses sing and spreading the tingling sensations all over.

"God, Jonas. I feel you everywhere."

His eyes glittered with satisfaction. "That's what I want. I want you to feel how much I love you so you'll always know."

And she *could* feel it, with every movement of his hips and every brush of his fingertips. Love was dripping all over them, and JJ wanted to roll in it until it was a permanent stain on her skin.

"I do feel it," she gasped. Then it was all too much, and the orgasm that had been building all along broke over her like a tidal wave. She slapped a hand over her mouth, trying to keep from screaming, but Jonas leaned up and swallowed the sound with his lips.

And as she broke apart, he put her back together with every touch.

———

Jonas called on all the strength he had to hang on through her orgasm. It was captivating to watch JJ when she was so vulnerable, a view that he was privileged to witness. And one he hoped he'd see multiple times before they were through.

It took a few minutes before she opened her eyes again. Her hair was flying all around her head, and her gorgeous blue eyes were glassy.

"You didn't..." she looked down at him in confusion.

Jonas pulled her forward until she collapsed on his chest. "Oh you didn't think I was going to let you off that easily, did you? I plan on keeping you up all night."

Her soft laugh puffed warm across his chest. "You're going to kill me! I can barely catch my breath."

Jonas flipped them, ignoring her squeal. He was going to get so much shit for this from the guys, but he didn't care.

JJ covered her eyes with her hands. "Did everyone hear me scream again? Tell me that was quiet."

Even though he'd just been having a similar thought, Jonas wasn't going to bullshit her. She was too smart for that anyway.

"Probably. But who cares? Hell, let them listen. Maybe they'll pick up a few pointers."

JJ giggled, her eyes shining. "I'll be sure to mention that to Oskar tomorrow morning."

That got a chuckle out of Jonas, too. "This whole situation is crazy but honestly, I'm grateful that we all ended up here. There's no one else I'd want watching my back in this situation."

She sobered instantly. "I know. Maybe that's how I need to look at things. That I'm exactly where I'm meant to be." Her fingers trailed through his hair and Jonas could have purred like a cat at the feeling.

"You're meant to be with me. I knew that the first time I heard that smart mouth."

"Like yours is any better." JJ opened her mouth to say something else, but the words dissolved into a soft sigh as he kissed her on the breastbone.

"What was that?" he asked innocently. Then he trailed his lips over the dents of her ribs and licked gently over her belly button.

"Nothing. I wouldn't want to distract you while you're busy." JJ's fingers tangled in his hair again and held him against her.

Jonas grumbled in appreciation as her legs fell open. One large hand on her abdomen held her still as he licked her clit delicately.

"Oh!" JJ shuddered so hard she almost dislodged his hand.

He fucking loved pleasuring her this way, surrounded by her warm, sugary, female scent and hearing her helpless little cries. There was no greater feeling of sexual mastery than to have your woman melting beneath your tongue and so lost in pleasure that she screamed your name.

He worked her faster, flicking her clit with the exact rhythm he knew would take her up quickly. Then just when she was about to fall over the edge, he throttled back, licking all around and kissing her mound gently. She let out a soft sound of disgruntlement but was soon whimpering again when he attacked her clit. He took her even higher and closer this time before backing off again.

JJ's fingers clenched in his hair so hard he saw stars. "What are you doing?"

"Easy, baby. It'll be even better if you work for it." He nipped at her belly and she moaned.

"I don't want to work for it. This is torture."

"Erotic torture." Jonas pushed a finger gently through the clenching muscles that were hungrily looking for something to grasp.

Her head fell back again. "Yes, just like that."

"I'm going to give you what you need. I'll always give you what you need," Jonas whispered, seeing how his soft words stoked her desire even higher. She nodded frantically as he continued whispering to her, and he saw the exact moment when she lost control.

And he cherished watching the only woman he'd ever truly loved.

JJ came down slowly, blinking sleepily at him. "You are entirely too good at that."

He grinned. "You definitely know how to make a guy feel good. But it's no hardship licking that sweet pussy, baby. I plan on making a meal of you every chance I can. So get used to screaming."

JJ covered her eyes with her hands but it didn't hide her red cheeks. "You know, Lucia said we're perfect for each other. She's totally right. Because I didn't think anyone had a mouth as filthy as mine!"

He grabbed another condom, cursing softly when he saw there was only one left. From now on, he was buying those things in bulk. He needed the lifetime supply because he was for damn sure going to be making love to her for at least that long.

The image of him as a randy eighty year old still chasing after JJ to squeeze her ass made him smile.

"You love me filthy."

JJ's satisfied smile was almost as good as an orgasm.

"You bet your ass I do."

CHAPTER FIFTEEN

The next few days they existed in a state of deliberate avoidance. JJ was busy pretending that the guys weren't plotting a dangerous mission to find her ex. Jonas pretended that the entire situation wasn't happening and made it a point to shower JJ with affection, reassurance and plenty of nights distracting her with sex so good that he didn't think she give a damn who heard her screaming.

But like all good things, it had to come to an end. JJ chewed her thumbnail next to Jonas as they watched Noah kissing Lucia goodbye.

"We're going to get this asshole, and then I'll be home before you wake up. Okay?" Noah stroked her face and looked into her eyes so intimately that Jonas was embarrassed to watch.

JJ turned to face Jonas. "I think this is a mistake."

He kept his face placid. This was a conversation they'd had many times over the past few days. Maybe she thought if she kept saying it, they'd change their approach. But they were following intel Matthias had found. JJ was upset that they were going in the opposite direction of Bliss, where she was pretty sure David would be hiding out. They'd already sent someone to check it out, but there was nothing there except a quiet town with friendly inhabitants.

"I know, baby. And I am going to look forward to saying 'I told you so' tomorrow morning."

"Wake me when you get in. I don't care how late it is," JJ insisted.

Jonas wasn't fooling himself that she would get any sleep anyway. More than likely she and Lucia would stay up, binge watch some shows on Netflix, and pretend they weren't both dying inside wondering if their men were okay. He understood because he understood how JJ worked. And he loved that she cared about him enough to worry, even if he hated to put her through this.

"Okay. I'll wake you."

"I still really think that you or Noah should have gone to Bliss to check things out. And you guys are going in the complete opposite direction."

Jonas nodded. "I know. But the trail is hotter where we're going. You know how good Matthias is at this stuff. He wouldn't lead us astray. This is our best chance to end this."

JJ sighed. "That's what I want. For this to be over and for things to go back to the way they used to be."

Lucia's voice interrupted from behind her. "You mean when I was running from a stalker and almost got kidnapped?"

JJ turned and accepted a hug from her friend. "I guess there's no normal for us, huh?"

"Probably not. But that's okay. I'll settle for safe and happy. Normal is boring."

Noah approached just then. Jonas could tell he was also armed to the teeth. Oskar appeared behind him with his grim face on. Dylan and Rafe stood at the doorway to the room but didn't enter. A few seconds later, Matthias appeared from down the hallway where his room was, dressed in all black and looking as lethal as Jonas had ever seen him.

"I guess it's time," JJ muttered. She turned to Jonas and hugged him tightly. Her softness pressed against his jacket, bumping against all the weapons underneath.

The thought of her pressing against all that metal sent a cold chill through him. What if this was the last time he'd ever get to hold her like this? His heart started racing, and he sucked in a desperate breath. He wished and prayed to a God he wasn't even sure he believed in before finally releasing her. Her arms slid from around his waist slowly. JJ didn't seem any more excited about letting go than he was, but at the same time, Jonas didn't want to leave her worried or upset.

This was going to be tricky enough as it was, even with a whole team going up against David. The thought of her upset would only distract him. They all needed to be on their A game tonight.

"Give me a kiss for luck," he whispered.

She leaned up to kiss him. Maybe she could read the worry in his eyes because she pasted on a smile and said, "Okay, I think Lucia and I are going to have a movie marathon."

Noah nodded at her appreciatively before kissing Lucia again. "That sounds good. Dylan will be watching over Nonna, just in case. Ryan will be here if you need anything."

"You mean he got stuck being our babysitter," Lucia teased.

Noah only smiled before motioning to the other guys. They all fell in line behind him as they left the room. Lucia grabbed her hand and squeezed hard. JJ clung to hers just as tightly.

Jonas turned back and walked up to JJ. "I just want you to know that we're not giving up. Even if this trail goes cold, we'll go check out Bliss. But no matter what, we'll get him. Okay?"

She nodded. "Okay. I trust you."

He kissed her quickly and then ran out after the others.

———

As soon as the door closed behind Jonas, Lucia let go of her hand. She turned to JJ with a gleam in her eye.

"We aren't really trusting them to do this, are we?"

JJ snorted. "Hell no. I just have no idea what to do yet. But we're definitely not going to sit here and watch movies like good little womenfolk, or whatever."

Lucia snickered. "Good. I was starting to get worried about you. Things are going to be tricky with Delaney here."

They both turned surreptitiously to look at Ryan. He was moving around the kitchen making a sandwich. When he felt both of their eyes on him, he paused and raised his eyebrows in question.

JJ waved prettily. "This is going to be a problem," she muttered out of the side of her mouth. "He might be younger, but all of these guys are paranoid as hell. It won't be easy to get around him."

Lucia hummed in agreement. "I know. But I think I have an idea. I just need to make a call."

While Lucia went to her room, JJ figured it would make the most sense to proceed as if the movie marathon was actually going to take place. She gathered several throw blankets and brought them to the couch then queued up

Netflix to a show that she'd never seen before. When Ryan looked up again, JJ walked to the kitchen.

"Do you want to share some popcorn with us?"

Ryan nodded. "Sure. What are you guys going to watch?"

Lucia came into the room with Isabella balanced on her hip. "Weren't we going to watch that breastfeeding documentary, JJ?" The innocent look on her face didn't waver as Ryan's expression changed to one of horror.

"*Oh, no.* That's okay. I'll let you two have some girl time." He snatched up his sandwich and left the kitchen.

A few seconds later, a door closed down the hallway. JJ burst into laughter. "You seriously just scarred the poor boy for life."

Lucia grinned. "Desperate times. If our plan is going to work, we need him off kilter."

"Plan? We have a plan now?"

"We do. Nonna is coming over to watch the baby and then we are going to go check out Bliss, Connecticut."

"Uh oh. When I said I wanted to do something, I didn't mean something that would put you in danger." JJ didn't want to lead her friend into trouble. She didn't want to think about Lucia exposed to David's special brand of crazy.

"Not me, but you'll put yourself in danger?" Lucia demanded. "No way. We've been friends a long time. If you wanted to keep me away from trouble, well I have to tell you, that ship sailed the day we met. And I wouldn't have it any other way."

JJ shook her head. "Noah is going to kill us. What am I saying? Jonas will too. That's if we can even get out of here. Ryan might allow Nonna to take the baby since Dylan is covering her. But there's no way he's going to let us walk out of here without him. Which means we're not getting anywhere near Bliss tonight."

Just then there was a knock on the door. Ryan came from the back immediately. If he was surprised to see them standing around talking instead of watching movies the way he'd expected, he didn't show it. After confirming who it was, he opened the door to a beaming Nonna.

"There's my *bambina!*" Nonna walked forward with her arms outstretched. Isabella let out a full belly laugh and tried to throw herself out of her mother's arms.

Ryan closed the door and then smiled at the older woman. Nonna had all of the men at Blake Security wrapped around her little finger. Or maybe mesmerized by the delicious homemade Italian food she brought over all the time.

"Ryan, I brought tiramisu. Dylan is bringing it up. I know how much you love it."

Ryan practically melted into a puddle of drool. "Tiramisu? I do love it. Thank you so much, Mrs. DeMarco."

Nonna rewarded him with a sweet smile. "I told you to call me Nonna."

Ryan nodded. "Yes, ma'am."

Dylan appeared then carrying an aluminum pan, and Ryan followed him to the kitchen. As soon as the men were out of hearing range, Nonna looked at the girls sternly.

"I expect you two to be careful. And watchful. I wouldn't help you if I didn't believe you would be."

"Yes, ma'am." JJ replied instinctively. No matter how old they got, Nonna DeMarco would always be the boss of them. "What is the plan, if you guys don't mind me asking?"

Lucia leaned forward. "Nonna brought the cake to distract Ryan. Now that we're all in the same place, Dylan will leave since he was technically supposed to be off duty tonight. Once he's gone, we'll trick Ryan into going into the panic room and then lock him in there."

JJ winced. "Damn, he's going to get in so much trouble."

Lucia looked uncomfortable, too. "I know. But I won't let Noah fire him. I don't care what I have to do."

Nonna raised her eyebrows. "That's enough about that, young lady."

They all chuckled together.

"Ok, so we just have to wait for Dylan and Ryan to come up with the idea of Dylan going home on their own. They aren't going to do it if we suggest it."

Nonna smiled slyly. "Don't worry about that. I took care of it."

"What do you mean you took care of it?" Lucia asked suspiciously.

They all froze at the sound of footsteps. Dylan and Ryan appeared. Ryan was holding a paper bowl filled with tiramisu and eating it noisily.

"Well, if you don't mind, I think I'll take off. Nonna fed me a really big dinner and I'm exhausted. Since she's planning to spend the night here so the girls can watch movies, we both don't need to be here, right?"

Ryan nodded, never taking his eyes off his cake. "Go on. You were supposed to be off anyway. Noah won't care. Matthias upgraded the security here, so once I turn the external alarms on, this place is safer than the Pentagon."

Dylan waved at them. "I'll see you ladies tomorrow then."

"Good night, dear!" Nonna called out. When she finally looked at Lucia and JJ and saw the looks on their faces, she huffed. "What? I may be old but I know how to knock a man out. *His stomach.* I stuffed that boy so full of gnocchi it'll be a wonder if he doesn't fall asleep before he makes it down the stairwell."

JJ was impressed. "Way to go, Nonna!"

Lucia glanced behind them. "One down, one to go."

To make their story more believable, they moved into the living room and turned on their Netflix show. Nonna bounced the baby on her lap and after an hour, JJ thought she'd lose her mind. What were they doing? Ryan had shown no sign of relaxing, she'd seen him upright typing on one of Matthias's spare computers when she'd gone to the bathroom.

Then Nonna stood and handed the baby to Lucia. "Young man! Yoo-hoo!"

JJ and Lucia exchanged confused looks but didn't move from their perch on the couch. Whatever Nonna was up to, they definitely weren't getting in her way.

"Yes, ma'am." Ryan appeared in the doorway to the room.

"I need your help carrying out the surprise present I brought for my granddaughter." Nonna marched down the hall, Ryan following.

Lucia leaned over. "She had Dylan bring in some big box when they came. But I'm not sure what that has to do with her plan."

A few moments later, there was a loud "Hey!" and then the sound of something crashing.

"What was that?" Lucia gasped. They both stood and rushed down the hallway toward Noah and Lucia's room.

JJ gaped at the scene. Nonna stood next to the panic room holding one of Lucia's fancy stilettos. A loud bang on the other side of the panic room door startled them all. Ryan's words were muffled, but it was easy to tell he was cursing up a storm in there.

"Oh, he is really upset with me," Nonna murmured.

"How did you get him in there?" Lucia asked

Nonna looked satisfied with herself. "I asked him to lift that big box. While his back was turned, I opened the panic room and then pushed him in. I disabled the lock pad with this!" she held up Lucia's shoe.

Suddenly she narrowed her eyes at them. "Now, before you go anywhere, you girls are taking weapons, right?"

JJ glanced behind her to see the keypad to the panic room was cracked. She looked back to Nonna with new eyes. "Wow. Remind me to never get on your bad side."

Nonna ambled over and patted her cheek. "There's no bad side for you, *cara*. You're family."

CHAPTER SIXTEEN

It took forever to get there.

At least that was how it seemed to Jonas. Noah took lead as usual, so he, Matthias and Oskar rode along. Rafe was right behind them, driving a second Jeep in case they should need alternate transportation out of there.

He didn't like to think of anything going wrong but after years of tactical training, it was second nature to prepare for the worst. Because no matter what, they were going home.

"Okay, so once we're there, Rafe goes in first. We'll hang back while he scouts. Once we have confirmation that

Chamaeleon is there, we go in hot. This shit ends tonight," Noah growled.

Matthias spoke up from the back. "All indications point to him crashing with an old friend in the Bronx. He tried to cover his tracks but several people in the neighborhood were able to ID him."

Jonas blew out a breath. "Good. This shit needs to end. Then we can go home."

Once they got closer, Rafe's Jeep split off and went down a different street. Noah pulled around until he found a quiet street where they could park. Once he cut the engine, it was still as a tomb.

"Well, hell. Somebody say something," Oskar finally drawled.

Noah cracked a smile. "You'd think I employed a bunch of kids. Shut the hell up so we can focus."

Oskar held up his hands. "Just trying to lighten the mood a bit."

Another few minutes went by in silence before Noah's phone beeped. "Yeah. What do you mean?"

Jonas rubbed his forehead, calling on all his strength not to snatch the phone from Noah's hand.

"No one's there?" Noah turned in his seat to stare at Matthias incredulously.

The kid paled slightly. "But I was so sure." He pulled out a laptop from somewhere and started typing frantically. "No, no, no. This morning when I checked there was a lease on file at this building for Ernest Fairway."

Jonas squinted, trying to remember. "Ernest is the guy David met while overseas, right?"

Matthias continued typing like a man possessed. "Yes. But now I see nothing in the landlord's system to indicate Fairway ever lived here at all."

Jonas slammed a fist into the dash. "*Motherfucker*! He's slipped right under our noses again. I promised JJ we'd get this sonofabitch. I promised her she'd be safe."

Noah's voice was soft, the kind you'd use to approach a wounded animal. "And you will. Jonas, listen to me. You will keep her safe. We all will."

Oskar's big beefy hand landed on Jonas's shoulder. "You know we've got your back."

He did know that. But at the moment that was poor consolation since the man terrorizing his woman was still out there and apparently about five steps ahead of them all the time. How the hell was he supposed to keep JJ safe when he wasn't entirely sure he could outsmart someone like David West? The dude was obsessed and diabolical, a bad combination. Not to mention, he had unlimited time to carry out his plans. None of them knew how long he'd been plotting this.

All they knew for sure was that West was obsessed with Rafe's life. And that ultimate obsession had also encompassed JJ. If he'd gone through the trouble to leave clues to lead them here, there must have been a reason.

"I need to call JJ. Make sure she's okay." He pulled his phone out and dialed her number. Every ring that went unanswered only ratcheted his fear higher.

"Nothing?" Noah asked. His brow furrowed and he pulled out his own phone.

Jonas watched as he finally hung up. "Lucia didn't answer either?"

"No. But they're probably just watching television and can't hear the phone. You know how Lucia likes to talk through every movie. Send Delaney a text. I'm sure they're fine."

Jonas blew out a breath. "Okay, first let's figure out where we went wrong tonight. Because I really don't want to go home with nothing."

Matthias saluted him. "On it. This might not be the right place, but we'll figure it out. He can't hide forever."

Jonas wasn't worried about Chamaeleon hiding forever because that didn't fit in with his goal. He was worried about him hiding long enough for JJ to relax her guard.

And then taking her away.

———

JJ peered over the steering wheel and tried to follow the directions Lucia called out.

"No, left here. And then down this street and one more right."

It was dark and there weren't that many streetlights. Her churning stomach combined with the absolute certainty that this was a really bad idea made it pretty difficult to navigate.

"This is it!" Lucia put her phone in her lap. "This is Rafe's old house."

JJ didn't park at the house, but instead kept driving and then circled around. They parked farther down the street. The house was an adorable little rambler. Exactly the kind of place that David had always talked about owning.

"Maybe we should call the guys," she finally said.

"Oh they already called," Lucia admitted.

"Wait, what? When?"

"While you were driving. I hit 'ignore' on both of our phones."

JJ shook her head. "I'm surprised they haven't sent out a search party for us." Then she winced. "They probably think we're okay since Ryan was with us."

Lucia sighed. "I do feel really bad about that part. But we had to do this. I'm not about to sit back while some psycho torments my best friend. And the guys didn't even listen when you told them about David wanting to live in Connecticut."

JJ knew she was right. If they'd left it up to the guys, they'd likely have missed any chance of nailing David before he moved to a new location. But they had to be careful about this. They'd just sneak up and take a look, enough to get hard proof he was there. Then they'd run like hell and call in the guys.

She was a strong, independent woman. But that didn't mean she was willing to put herself in danger to prove it. The guys had way more experience with this kind of thing. She and Lucia could restrict themselves to the surveillance portion of the security business.

"Okay, did you bring the binoculars?"

"Yes! I did. These are some new, heat sensing type binoculars that Noah was really excited about. I also grabbed this!" Lucia held up the gun she'd taken from the weapons room.

JJ held up a hand. "Okay, let's save that for hopefully never. This is not going to be some kind of female James Bond-Charlie's Angels situation. We are going to spy on him, but I don't plan on getting anywhere close to David ever again."

"Of course. I just brought it because... well, you never know. Rafe taught me that." Lucia put the gun back and handed JJ one of the heat sensing binoculars.

She trained it on the house down the street. Nothing.

"Are they supposed to light up or do something?"

Lucia put her pair to her face. "I'm not sure. I hate to say it, but we probably need to be closer."

JJ gulped. "Okay, let's get out. Leave the car open so we can run back and jump inside quickly if we need to. But we'll walk up the street and see if we can detect anyone inside. If no one is there, we might be doing all of this for nothing."

Lucia took off her seatbelt. "I don't think it's for nothing. At least we're checking out a valid lead. If he's not here, it gives Matthias one less place to focus on."

They left the car unlocked and closed the doors as quietly as possible. It was a bright night, the moon shining directly overhead, making up for the lack of streetlights. The house in question only had one light on up front, and there were no cars in the driveway.

"What if he drives up while we're walking by?" Lucia whispered.

JJ had just had a similar thought. "Keep an eye out behind us. If you see anyone driving up, we can knock on one of these other doors and pretend we're lost or something."

Luckily no one drove up or down the street as they were walking. JJ raised her binoculars and pointed them at the house. She pulled the binoculars down with a frown. "Are these supposed to do something? I don't see anything."

Lucia shrugged. "I think you're supposed to see things change color when they detect heat."

"Well, if that's true then no one is here. I don't see anything."

"Oh, dang. I really want to get some proof so we can get the guys to take this seriously. I wasn't expecting to actually see him or anything, but a sign would be nice," Lucia complained.

JJ couldn't help but laugh at that. "A sign that says "super secret psycho man's hideout?"

"Yes. Exactly like that," Lucia added.

JJ wasn't sure what came over her but before she knew it she was marching toward the house. No one was there, she'd already seen that. So it wasn't that big of a deal to get closer and look inside. Maybe they'd see something that could prove David was there if they took a quick look. But she was tired of waiting and worrying about when he'd pop up. This might be her only chance to outsmart him.

"JJ, what are you doing?" Lucia whispered frantically as she followed JJ around to the back of the house.

"He used to always say he'd hide his keys under a planter," JJ muttered. Then just like she'd conjured it, she saw it. A huge planter right by the back door. She lifted it and took out the small silver key underneath.

"You aren't going–"

"Inside. Yes, I am," JJ stated before Lucia could even finish. "For once we're ahead in this twisted game, and I'm not going to let this opportunity pass me by. You can wait in the car if you want."

Lucia punched her arm. "I'm not leaving you. I'll keep a lookout while you search the place. Plus, I brought this. Just in case, remember?" She held up the gun.

JJ blew out a breath. "Okay, let's do this."

She opened the back door with the key and then paused, listening. It was quiet and still. They moved through the house quickly, not wasting any time. Lucia posted herself by the back window while JJ searched the front room. There were piles of mail on the side table addressed to

Charlie Townsend. Another alias? Then she lifted the cushions of the couch to see if he'd hidden anything there.

A soft sound behind her made JJ freeze in place. But when she turned, nothing was there.

"Lucia!" she hissed into the shadows.

Then one of the shadows moved and formed a familiar shape.

"David," she breathed.

CHAPTER SEVENTEEN

"Jesus, Ryan, what the hell is up?"

"What the hell is up is that I've been calling you the last two hours. Reception in here sucks."

Jonas sighed and pinched the bridge of his nose. "Sorry we went radio silent. "What's up? Is everyone okay?"

"No, everyone is *not* okay. The girls, they fucking locked me in the panic room."

Jonas shook his head. "Wait a sec, let me conference Rafe in."

After pushing a few buttons, Rafe answered with a grumbled "What?"

Jonas put the phone on speaker so everyone in the car could hear. "Okay, Delaney repeat that."

"They locked me in the panic room. Lucia, and JJ. And Nonna. Fucking old lady helped."

Next to him, Noah sat up straight. "What did Nonna do? Where the hell is Isabella?"

Ryan's exasperation was clear on the other end of the line. "That's what I'm trying to tell you. Lucia had the old woman come over to spend time with the baby. Since they were all in one place, Dylan went home. Next thing I know, Nonna asked me to carry something in your room for her. I went in to help her, and before I knew it, she'd shoved me in the panic room and did something to the lock so I can't reset it. I'm locked in here. Fucking battery's dying to boot."

Jonas stared at the phone and then lifted his gaze to Noah. "You know, I wish I could say I was surprised, but I'm sure this was Lucia and JJ's idea."

Noah chuckled. "You might be surprised. Nonna is a pistol. Hey Rafe, any idea what your grandmother is up too?"

Rafe's voice grumbled over the line. "No idea. But we

need to find those girls. Isabella is safe. Nonna would never risk her safety. So we just have to find the girls."

Oskar shook Matthias awake. The kid jerked, and his right hand immediately went to palm one of his blades. "Easy, kid. Need your hacking skills not your slicing skills."

Matthias blinked for several seconds as if trying to orient himself before he nodded. "Yep, on it." He pulled out his laptop. "What am I looking for?"

"You're looking for Lucia and JJ."

Matthias frowned. "I was out for all of five minutes. What the hell happened to them now?"

Jonas shook his head. "I don't think something happened to them, I think *they* happened to Delaney. For some reason they wanted out of the penthouse. So they locked him in the panic room."

A slow grin spread over Matthias's lips. "No shit?"

Noah chuckled even as he made a left turn. "No shit. Can you track down the girls? I just hope both of them haven't forgotten everything I've ever said about safety and have left their damn phones on."

"Even if they have, Lucia has likely forgotten about the tracker you stuck in her purse. So we can find them that way."

Jonas blinked his eyes in amazement. "Noah, you're still tracking Lucia even after she found out last year?"

Noah didn't look the slightest bit sheepish. "Well, I wasn't. And then that idiot took my baby. So I turned the tracking back on."

Jonas chuckled. "Man, I hope we find them. Because I want to see the look Lucia gives you when she finds out that you're still tracking her movements."

"Man, shut up. You worry about your woman, and I'll worry about mine."

"Yeah, if only that was the way it worked. Because the moment you start yelling at yours for pulling a stunt this stupid, mine's gonna jump on the bandwagon and start chewing your ass out."

Noah grumbled. "Yeah, you're right about that."

Matthias pulled up their location and cursed softly under his breath. "I have them. Neither one of you is gonna like where they are."

"Out with it, Matthias," Jonas prompted.

"Bliss, Connecticut. Looks like they've gone hunting on their own."

Rafe cursed. "They've gone to my old house."

Matthias nodded. "I guess JJ got fed up with us not looking into it."

Jonas took the laptop out of the kid's hand and stared at the monitor. "Oh, for the love of Christ."

Lucia and JJ had gone after Chamaeleon on their own.

"**I** knew you'd come back. I bought this house for you."

JJ backed away. "David. You don't want to do this."

"Do what? Have you? You are mine. I was sent away for a while. But, I'm back now. And there's no reason we can't be together."

JJ frantically searched for a weapon. Something. Anything. Lucia had the gun. She hadn't wanted anything to do with it. So all she had was a nail file in her back pocket as part of the lock picking kit they'd brought. Such a dumb idea. What made them think they could be in and out and he wouldn't notice?. What the hell had she been thinking? *You were thinking about keeping Jonas safe.* What skills did she have?

You are Jessica freaking Jones. You are smart. Think your way through this. He wants you. He's not going to hurt you. Lucia was protected because she had her gun. Which meant JJ just had to keep him talking until Lucia could shoot him. Yeah okay that was a plan. Maybe not the most thought-out one she'd ever had, but hey, in a pinch it wasn't bad.

Maybe not, but you do have your phone. And one thing she was good at was texting with her eyes closed. She put her hands behind her back even as she stepped backward trying to keep him talking. "David, listen to me. We don't want to do this. You and I, we don't work. You weren't happy with me anyway. I never made you happy."

"I decide what makes me happy. And it's not about happiness. I *own* you."

JJ hoped she'd managed to unlock her phone and had found the app properly by memory. Lucia was the last person she'd texted, so she should get the message. *Send help. He's got me in the kitchen.*

"Why did you have to do it? Hook up with that guy? He's weak. He's not as strong as I am."

"He's stronger than you are. He's a better man. He's kinder, and I love him. And he's better in bed." Okay, maybe that was going too far, but the truth was the truth.

David lunged for her, and she scooted out of the way. But she wasn't fast enough and he managed to grab her by the wrist, hauling her up against him. Then he grabbed the front of her dress and lifted her easily off the ground. "You were always such a lying whore. You know I'm the best you've ever had or ever will have again. *I am Rafe fucking DeMarco.*"

JJ blinked at him. Jesus, he'd lost it. Having her call him Rafe during sex was twisted enough but he really believed that he was Rafe. That was —sick. Yeah, any way she looked at this, they had arrived at cray-cray town.

"You are going to live here, and you're going to be my wife. We are going to raise children in this house. Just like the life you always wanted with me. We're going to live in the house I grew up in. I'm going to have the one thing that he couldn't have."

"You've got it wrong. I didn't love Rafe. He was a crush. This obsession you have, you can't see the truth. Rafe and me... we were never a thing. Your obsession with him, it's why you sought me out. Lucia was too broken. But I was the perfect target. I know this isn't about me. This is about Rafe."

"No, no, no, no." He pressed her up against the wall, and she tried to struggle out of his grip. "*I* am Rafe. We are going to have children in this house. Two of them, and we're even going to name them Rafe Jr. and Lucia."

"You're a sick bastard."

"I'll be as sick as you want. Is that what you're into now? You know I bugged Castillo's apartment, right? You like being controlled. I know that much. You like being told what to do, you like being dominated, you like having control stripped away."

"You're an asshole of the lowest order. I hate everything about you."

He bared his teeth, and she could see the fury written all over his face. He banged her against the wall, and pain ricocheted through her skull, making her teeth ache. Somewhere in the back of her mind, the self-preservationist part of her brain told her to be quiet. To stop talking. To not make it any worse. But she couldn't help it. "You realize you're a little-dick motherfucker right? Shit, I have balls bigger than yours. The fact that you have to scare and terrorize a woman to make her be with you makes you pathetic. It makes you sad."

Again he banged her against the wall. *Fuck that hurt.*

And then she saw a flicker from the dining room. She could only hope, she could only pray that it was help. So she kept him distracted. "Do you know that every time we had sex, I used to imagine it was Rafe? I mean I didn't know what sex could be, and all I really wanted was that loved feeling, but I hated having sex with you. Every single time, it was awful. God knew I never once, *not once*, had an orgasm. And you know what? All Jonas has to do is look at me, and orgasm is imminent. You could never do that. Because you're half the man he is. Hell, you want to borrow my brass balls for a second?"

He lifted her again, ready to bang her head into the wall. But then his grip eased on the front of her dress, and JJ's feet hit the ground. David sagged, and Lucia stood over him holding a metal pipe. "That's for taking my baby."

JJ met her gaze. "Oh my God. I cannot believe you did that. Although, that's what I call laying pipe."

Lucia stared at the metal in her hand, her lips twitching with a hint of a smile. "I think he's been living in the basement. It's where I found this. There's only one room with anything in it. I couldn't figure how to get the safety off the damn gun, so I had to get closer. I'm sorry. Are you okay?" She reached for JJ, and JJ winced.

"I am, let's get out of here."

But as JJ stumbled over his body heading for the dining room and the front door, David grabbed Lucia's ankle. "You're not going anywhere."

Lucia went sprawling, and so did the pipe and the gun. "JJ, take those. Run."

The hell she was running without her best friend. JJ picked up the gun and checked the safety. It was jammed. With all her might, she pushed up to release it and heard the click. Then she aimed. God, the last thing on Earth she wanted to do was hit Lucia. And Lucia was putting up one hell of a fight. Elbows, knees, biting, scratching. There was blood everywhere. But when David had her best friend pinned down with his hand on her throat, JJ didn't even think. She just fired.

The loud crack reverberated throughout the room. But she didn't stop there.

She remembered every single time he'd ever lifted his hand to hit her, every single time he'd ever held her down and ignored her protests about how she didn't want to sleep with him. She remembered every single time she'd been made to cower, every single time he'd deliberately hurt her, and she fired again. *Crack.* She thought about all the things he'd said to her about how she was pathetic and sad, and the times he'd told her that she wasn't beautiful. *Crack.* She'd fired a bullet into his chest, one in his shoulder, and another in his neck, but the rage was still in his eyes as he continued to choke her best friend.

Terror shook JJ's body as she spoke. "I only came here to tell you to stop. This has to end. You don't have to die today."

He sneered at her then stared down at Lucia. And Lucia just gasped for breath. "I will never stop."

She knew he wasn't lying, that every word out of his mouth was the truth. Then with calm in her heart, she released another bullet. That one got him between the eyes. And then he fell forward on top of Lucia.

CHAPTER EIGHTEEN

Jonas was frantic.

It baffled him that anything got done over the next hour because his brain felt like it had been through a blender. His entire universe had realigned in the space of just a few seconds.

JJ was out there, possibly in danger, and he was too far away to help.

"Can't we go any faster?" he barked at Noah, who was currently driving the car practically at warp speed. The look his friend shot at him would have turned a lesser man to stone. As it was, Jonas felt his balls shrivel a few sizes.

"I know where your head is at, brother." Noah said in a deceptively calm voice. "My woman is out there, too. You know I'm going as fast as I can without this Jeep growing wings."

Jonas took a deep breath and then another. Attacking the people on his side wasn't helping the situation. Plus, he knew how they all felt about JJ and Lucia. Those women were special to each of them in different ways. There was no other team more invested in bringing them home safely. But still, they didn't have their entire lives wrapped up in this outcome. Well, Noah did. But the others, they had no idea. Until you felt that way about someone, you couldn't understand how their safety and happiness was the key to everything being all right in your world.

"There's a chance we're panicking for nothing," Noah continued. "Lucia wouldn't put them in direct danger, not after all of the safety lectures she's gotten from me. If anything, they're probably just driving around that area looking for clues."

"Maybe," Jonas hedged. But in his heart, he knew that if his JJ was out there, she wasn't hiding in the car. Crazy woman that she was, she wouldn't approach with caution, she'd charge straight into trouble and tell everyone there to go to hell.

Jesus.

"What the hell were they thinking?" he muttered.

"I hate to be the voice of reason," Matthias began. "But they were probably pissed that we didn't investigate the information JJ offered more thoroughly."

"Well, why the hell didn't we?" Jonas roared.

Was he having a heart attack? It felt like the damn organ was bouncing around in his chest like it wanted out. Everything was out of control and he wasn't sure exactly what he was supposed to be doing. All he knew was that whatever he did might not be enough.

Because he knew what kind of trouble Jessica Jones was capable of getting into.

Oskar's meaty hand landed on his shoulder, probably the only thing strong enough to keep him from launching out of the seat.

"We've always done the best we could with the information we had at the time. It didn't seem likely that Chamaeleon would be hiding out playing house in some sleepy little Connecticut town. But seeing how crafty this dude is, maybe that's why it makes sense. He's always doing what we don't expect."

"And information changes," Matthias interjected. "Because when I searched before, there was nothing to indicate that Chamaeleon was there. But I just got the utilities records back, and Rafe's old house is drawing more power than it should considering that the owners are out of the country."

Jonas swiveled in his seat. "Shouldn't there be *no* power if no one is currently living there?"

"There's always a residual amount drawn as long as the power is connected. But there are spikes here at night, which definitely indicate that someone is using it. Could be squatters but..." Matthias shrugged.

"But you don't think so?" Jonas pressed.

"With this new information, the fact that the other hideout is empty, and his obsession with Rafe, I don't think so. I think he's been there for a while, plotting."

"And JJ tried to tell us." Jonas rubbed a hand over his face. If he couldn't get to her in time, he would never forgive himself. She'd tried to tell them. She'd trusted them to protect her.

No, she trusted you to protect her. And you let her down.

"What the hell are we walking into?" Jonas asked.

"It could be anything. Maybe we've taken him off guard and this will be a quick, in-and-out, take-him-out operation," Oskar answered.

"Or?" Jonas was almost afraid to ask about the other option. Because he had a gut feeling that the "or" included JJ and Lucia putting themselves in danger.

Or was not something he was prepared to face.

Apparently Oskar felt the same way. "Let's hope 'or' doesn't happen. We need to find this dude and fast. Before he realizes that JJ and Lucia are looking for him."

Noah slowed as they exited the highway and entered the small town of Bliss. From what Jonas knew, there wasn't a whole lot to the place. Small country ramblers, a general store, a few mom and pop stores, and a whole lot of fields. Not the kind of place where you'd expect a psychotic, ex-secret agent with a weird bro-crush to reside.

"We're going to proceed with the same amount of caution

we'd use under any other circumstances," Noah stated with a pointed look for Jonas. "Going in with guns blazing could backfire if he's got the girls."

Rationally, Jonas knew he was right. But it didn't quell the urge to palm two guns and bust through the door in a blaze of glory.

"We'll be tight," Oskar assured Noah. "I just texted Rafe to approach from behind as usual. Then we can go in the front and fan out in teams of two."

They all checked their gear as Noah parked down the block. In addition to all the guns, they were all fitted with in-ear comms. From a distance, the house in question was dark and looked completely unassuming. Jonas made a signal to Noah that he would fall behind as they approached, the only sound the barely detectable whisper of their boots over the grass.

"Front door is locked." Oskar's soft murmur came over the comms. A few seconds later, they heard Rafe confirm that the back door was open.

Noah pointed at Matthias and Oskar to remain at the front and then headed for the back, with Jonas right behind. There were no lights on, but they all had excellent night vision. Jonas could easily make out the shape of

Noah right in front of him, and then once they turned a corner in the house, Rafe ahead of him.

Movement to their right had them all swinging their weapons in that direction.

"Hands up!" Rafe commanded.

Feminine screams erupted.

"JJ?" Jonas asked.

"Oh my god! It's you!" JJ dropped what she was holding. "I'm so glad you're here. We didn't know what to do!"

He heard Noah's voice over the comms letting Oskar and Matthias know it was safe to come in. But the only thing he could focus on was what JJ had been holding. As soon as she stepped back, he could see what it was. David West's arm.

"Holy shit. Is that—" Rafe stared incredulously.

"David? Yes, he's dead. I shot him." JJ huffed. "We were trying to figure out how to get him out of here."

"I thought we could wheel him out in this suitcase," Lucia continued, gesturing to an oversize brown suitcase next to her. "But it turns out he's way heavier than he looks. So it's a good thing you guys are here. This part sucks."

Rafe burst into laughter and glanced over at Noah. "This is what you've done to my sister? I raised a perfect angel, and now she's hiding dead bodies?"

Noah snickered. "She's a DeMarco. What the hell do you expect?"

"Um, hello?" Lucia screeched. "Dead guy at two o'clock. Are you guys going to help us get rid of this or what? Because I need to get home and feed the baby. Nonna will be expecting to hear from us soon."

JJ grinned. "That's right. And I'm sure she'll want to know her plan went off perfectly."

"Her plan?" Rafe repeated.

"Of course. Nonna is quite the mastermind." JJ took great pleasure in watching all the guys' shocked expressions.

Men always thought they had the women in their lives figured out. Well, no one was ever going to put her in a box. She hoped to be just as gutsy and causing as much trouble as Nonna in her older years.

Her eyes landed on Jonas. More than anything, she hoped to be causing trouble with him.

"Take me home, please," she whispered.

"You got it, baby." Jonas pulled her close and kissed her forehead. "After this stunt you'll be lucky if I ever let you out of the bed again. At least I know you're safe there."

JJ smiled. If he thought she was safe in bed, he had no idea what he was in for. She planned to cause just as much trouble in the bedroom as she did everywhere else.

———

Matthias watched everyone leave.

JJ was being unusually docile as she allowed Jonas to lead her out the door. He overheard something about never letting her out of bed again, which he ignored. No more mental images of those two were needed. Some of the things he'd overheard lately could never be forgotten. It was a wonder he could look anybody he lived with in the face these days.

Speaking of PDA, his boss was currently trying to be stern with his wife, while Lucia was pretending to listen. The smile on her face pretty much said 'I'll play nice for a while but in the end, I do what I want.' As sweet as she was, Lucia was surprisingly headstrong. Oh, she'd keep a smile on her face the whole time, but no man controlled her. It was one of the things Matthias had always liked about her.

A woman like that would fight by your side through anything.

"Sorry to put you on cleanup duty, Matthias." Noah actually did look apologetic, not something he did often. But it was no real secret that Noah and the others tried to shield him from anything too grim.

Matthias cringed. He hated that anyone knew so much about him, about the things he'd done. It was weird knowing that they were all watching, expecting him to go off the rails if he was exposed to anything too dark.

He didn't need to be coddled. He pulled his weight. Always had. Probably more than his fair share.

"It's all good, guv. You know I can handle things."

Noah smiled at the slang term for *boss*. He'd always found the British way of speaking amusing. Matthias loved to remind him that Yankee slang was just as strange.

"Good. Call me as soon as the ORUS man comes through." Noah saluted as he led Lucia out.

He didn't let out a breath until the door closed behind

them. Then he turned to survey the grim scene left behind in the house. With his training, he could see exactly how things had played out.

Chamaeleon on the ground, maybe on his knees? JJ must have been standing over him to get that angle. He knelt slightly to examine the bullet wound in the former David West's forehead.

Dimly, Matthias was aware that this was a little twisted. Some of the most cold-blooded agents he'd worked with had been a little squeamish about getting close to the dead, but it had never bothered him. Hell, the hard part was over at that point. It was actually rather fascinating, how someone could be alive in this world in one second and then gone the next.

He supposed it was a by-product of seeing so much death in his life that it fascinated him so.

Once he heard the Jeep pull away, Matthias pulled out his phone to wait. Once Noah made contact with the head of ORUS, they'd be sending a cleaner out. It wasn't exactly glamorous work, but someone needed to be here to oversee things and make sure nothing was missed. They couldn't afford any aspect of ORUS's fuckup to blow back on them later. The girls being here added another layer of complication to things, because they didn't have the training to conceal the forensic evidence of being here. After the grim work was done, Matthias would go over every inch of this place until there was no trace that JJ or Lucia had been there.

That anyone had been there.

He killed an hour playing a puzzle game on his phone before he got the message from Noah that ORUS was sending someone. Another hour went by before he heard someone at the front door. Reflex had his gun in his hand before he could even blink. The man who stepped through the door was unfamiliar but completely recogniz-able. Hair shorn close, non-descript clothes, blank eyes.

Matthias figured he was probably just as predictable.

"You're the cleaner?"

The man nodded once and turned his arm slowly to reveal his wrist. The small pattern of dots revealed were similar to the ones that Matthias still sported, as did Noah and Rafe. The symbol of a grim brotherhood.

"Good. Let's get started. There's a lot of blood and I want a completely clean sweep of this place."

The other man nodded. "This is going to take a while."

Matthias pushed up his sleeves, ready to get to work. He didn't mind if it took all night if it meant JJ and Lucia were protected. It was something he could give back to the people who had become his family. They thought he was standoffish and distant, but if they only knew where he'd started... Emotionally, he'd given them the very best he was capable of giving.

Whatever was left of his heart was theirs, even if they didn't know it.

CHAPTER NINETEEN

As soon as they arrived home, Jonas dragged JJ into the living room and wrapped his arms around her. "Jesus Christ do you know how happy I am to have you home safe? I was too terrified to believe it in the car. But with you home, it's more real now."

JJ snuggled into Jonas's embrace. "Let me guess, you're not letting me out of your sight for a while?"

"Woman, can you really blame me? I mean you girls fucking locked Ryan in the panic room."

"Well, it's not like he was gonna let us go willingly. He would've called you and you would've talked us out of it and said you had it handled. But you had the wrong location. None of you were listening."

"Okay, okay I hear you. Next time let's have a code word for when I'm being an idiot and not listening and you're about to do something stupid to get my attention."

"It wasn't intended to be like that. It's not like I was an idiot exactly. We had a weapon."

Jonas shuddered. She could feel the shiver run through his body. "Yeah, I know. I just hate to think of what would have happened if he'd have gotten a hold of it. If Lucia hadn't been there. All these horrible things were running through my head a million times today. Do you understand that?"

She nodded. "Yeah, I understand. And I'm sorry."

"I know. Listen, let's do first things first."

JJ cocked her head. "Seriously, you want to have sex now?"

Jonas stared at her for a long moment. And then chuckled. "Yes, actually. But that's not what I meant."

Behind them, there was a giggle. Noah had his arms wrapped around Lucia and lifted his gaze and met

Jonas's. "Listen, I need to have a conversation with my wife about her antics today. We'll need about an hour. Make sure Nonna's okay with the baby, and get Delaney out of the panic room would you?"

"Yeah, Delaney. That was actually my first stop."

Noah blinked at him like he was crazy. "Yeah, okay. But uh, Lucia is my first stop."

Lucia rolled her eyes and swatted him on the arm before following her husband as he tugged her down the hall into his office. JJ would've loved for that to be her first stop. But honestly, she was still reeling and shaking, and she didn't know what she felt or how she should be feeling. All she felt right now was numb and hollow. And God, she just wanted to collapse. She'd killed a man today. Shot him dead. Several times. *But he was going to kill Lucia if you hadn't.*

She might act tough, but that shell she put up for the world to see, it didn't mean she didn't care. It didn't mean she wasn't affected by things. Jonas pulled her close and hugged her tight. "I know. You're in shock. Let's get you in the shower, I'll deal with Delaney. And then I'll call Oskar and Dylan and have them escort Nonna back to the penthouse."

She shook her head. "No. I need to let out Ryan. I feel like we owe him one."

Jonas studied her carefully. "Are you okay?"

"Yes. No. I have no idea."

Jonas nodded. "I know it couldn't have been easy doing what you did today. I know how terrifying it must have been."

"That's just the thing, Jonas. When I saw him hurting my friend, I didn't even think twice. I might have emptied the whole clip into him at the end there. I just kept shooting."

"And that's what you're supposed to do. You reacted to save your friend."

"Yeah. I know. But I also reacted to save myself."

"That is a good thing. Because for once, you thought about survival. I'm proud of you." He took her hand and pulled her down the hall until they reached the panic room. Then he pushed the combo into the keypad. When the door unlatched, Delaney was hanging by his hands in the doorjamb, looking pissed and ready to kill someone.

"Are you fucking serious right now? We will never speak of this again, do you understand?"

JJ opened her mouth to apologize. She really meant to. But instead, what came out was, "What's the matter Delaney afraid of the dark? Or are you pissed off that three little women outsmarted you?"

Delaney opened his mouth and then snapped it shut. "I was worried because I was on Isabella duty. I don't think having two men on her and Nonna is enough."

JJ grinned at him. "I am sorry. But I knew you would've stopped us."

"Damn straight I would've stopped you. You could've been killed. You could've gotten Lucia killed. And then Noah would have killed us all."

She nodded. "I know. I know it was stupid. But I had to do something. I'm so sorry that you got caught up in it."

It took him several beats, but then he nodded.

Within fifteen minutes, Dylan and Oskar were back with Nonna and Isabella. Nonna, for her role in all this, acted as if everything was fine. She just smiled and gave JJ a kiss on the cheek. "Oh, JJ. It's good to see you again. We had a lovely walk out in the park, didn't we boys?"

Both Dylan and Oskar looked a little worse for wear. As if

Nonna'd had them running for their lives. She was really going to have to ask the old lady what she'd done to them. Either way, everyone looked safe and happy.

Isabella must have known she was home though and that her parents were home as well, because the moment the stroller came to a stop she let out a tiny wail, which of course drew Lucia and Noah out of the office. Both of them had bed hair. And Lucia had that sort of satisfied, smug look on her face that screamed 'Hey, I just had sex with my husband.'

"Oh my, sweetheart. Mama's here."

With Isabella in Lucia's arms, JJ watched on. Lucia had saved her life today. *And you saved hers.* "Can a godmother get a kiss too? I know you're hungry little one. But I just want one little baby kiss." She kissed her goddaughter and was never more grateful for the family that she had.

Noah inclined his head for the guys to follow him to the conference room. "Hey guys, let's get this over with and call Ian."

Jonas followed, but he grumbled. "I can't believe we're still going to deal with that guy."

Noah was philosophical about it. "Look, we're not necessarily going to be friends, but we don't need to be enemies. Besides, now he owes us. And I've a feeling with this bunch we'll be collecting on that favor sometime soon."

———

Matthias had to get the hell out of the penthouse. It was too much. All of it. All the happy couples. He left without a word, but Oskar saw him going.

When the German gave him a quizzical glance, Matthias just ignored him. After everything that had happened in the last couple of days, he was still feeling raw. The monster inside him was too close to the surface, and he needed to take the beast out for a walk away from the people he cared about. And he needed to put his past to bed.

Something happened to him at that house. The moment his hands had grasped those blades, he'd started to enjoy the fight. It was one thing to go hand-to-hand combat, it was another thing to actually use his weapon of choice. Knives were personal. And he'd enjoyed it a little too much. Now stuffing the monster back inside was a little more difficult to do. Especially since he'd been out to play in spectacular fashion.

Matthias followed the directions to the letter. He took the train downtown to the meet point, across the street from Club Throb. In the small neighborhood park he took the bench facing the club and waited silently for the rest of his party to show up. There was no running away now.

Matthias felt more than heard when the bench behind him was occupied. "I told you your past was coming for you. But it's here. I've had a sighting."

Matthias sighed. "Do you know if they know where to find me?"

"Not yet. But given that your boss is so tight with Orion, it might only be a matter of time. They knew where to start looking. So I'm not sure how much time you've got."

"Well, if they come looking, they're going to find trouble."

"Are you going to tell them?"

There was something that he'd thought about long and hard. What did he tell Noah? He'd never really disclosed all of his past, just given him bits and pieces that were enough to form his own version of the story.

Although what Noah had formed already had been the stuff of nightmares. But real life was so much worse. Bad enough to give the devil himself nightmares.

Before he'd come into ORUS, he'd been barely human. A real-life Dr. Jekyll and Mr. Hyde. Orion had flipped a switch inside him that made everything go from terrible to monstrous.

He had to keep them all safe from himself. Which included keeping them safe from this. "I'm not telling them anything. It's my mess. My past. I want to protect them as long as I can."

"Matthias, if your old family is looking for you, then you probably need to warn Leo at the very least."

"Not going to happen. I will protect them. That's what you do for family. Protect them and keep them safe. That's my job."

"Mate, if you're not gonna warn them, there's not much I can do to help you."

Matthias ground his teeth. "If anyone comes knocking at my door, they're not going to be happy about it."

"What do you need? I feel like I need to do something. I owe you my life."

Matthias thought a minute. "Nothing. We're done. You've done enough. Debt is paid. You come knocking on my door again, and I'm going to assume that you're with them. And we both know what I do to enemies."

"**I** need you to put this on."

JJ leaned against the SUV and stared at him. "You know I'm not into bondage."

Jonas's smile was wolfish. "Now, let's not tell lies. You're in for a little blindfold fun, and you liked it when I restrained you that one time."

JJ flushed. Which, considering who she was, and who they were together, was a hard feat. "Okay, you might have a point there. But I'm still not wearing a blindfold."

"Come on, it's a surprise. I thought you loved surprises."

JJ let her gaze slide down the straining cotton of his T-shirt, down his taut, chiseled abs, and then to his belt. She very deliberately gave him a devious smile. "I like surprises."

Jonas groaned and then planted his hands on either side of her, barricading her against the SUV. "Woman, we just made it out of the penthouse. I would actually like to go forward with the surprise. But if you keep looking at me like that, we won't leave. I'll drag you back upstairs to our room, and do all sorts of naughty things to you. And then our surprise will be delayed. We'll probably get there at night, and you won't be able to see it properly."

"You say that like it's a bad thing. Besides, maybe I'll distract you and you'll forget all about this surprise that requires me to wear a blindfold."

He bent and nuzzled her neck, and she could feel herself melting. He was too good at that. *Far too good.* Matter of fact, if he kept that up, she pretty much would give him anything he wanted. Oh, the possibilities.

"I will not be persuaded by kisses."

"Come on. I'm just asking to give you a surprise. Let me give you something. You trust me don't you?"

JJ giggled because she could feel his smile on her skin. She could be gracious, she could do this. Give him a little leeway and let him think he had the upper hand. Because, let's face it, they both knew she had the upper hand. She had boobs. And ass. Boobs and ass trumped everything when it came to men and women.

"Okay," she dissented. "You can blindfold me."

He immediately pulled back and gave her wolfish grin. "Really? That was way too easy. I anticipated a lot convincing. You know, driving you to the brink of orgasm, refusing to let you come until you said you'd let me blindfold you, and then keeping you on the verge of coming until we got to your surprise."

She narrowed her gaze at him. He knew what he was doing. His words alone were enough to make her hot. "I've been teaching you too much."

"Hey, I'm still trying to pay you back for that little trip to Vegas a month ago."

JJ had to smile at that. She had worked with the guys to secure a private jet so they could spend a couple of nights in Vegas. On the plane ride there, she'd handcuffed him to his seat and then given him a private lap dance and tortured him until he pretty much begged her to come. "You know what? You enjoyed every moment of that."

His gaze narrowed, and the flash of heat was instant. God she really did want to drag him upstairs. Fine, so maybe she was just as susceptible to him as he was to her.

"Maybe."

"Maybe I take you upstairs and remind you."

He shook his head. "Too late now. You've already agreed to let me blindfold you. Turn around."

"You want my hands on the car. Are you going to arrest me officer?"

As she turned around, he groaned low. "You are pretty much playing to every single dirty fantasy I've ever had about arresting a hot woman."

"You want to play cops and robbers?" She added a seductive note to her voice. Behind her Jonas just chuckled as he delicately placed the blindfold over her eyes and tied a knot securely at the back of her head.

When she blinked, she realized she could still see some light. So not total darkness. Besides, he was right. She might fight him on things like this, but when it came down to it, if he said jump she would ask how high. Because he would never hurt her. And he would annihilate anyone else who tried. He'd already proven that.

"Naughty robbers get spankings, JJ."

"Oh, you're scaring me now, Officer Castillo," she said.

His voice was low and husky with just a hint of bite. "That's Detective Castillo to you."

JJ giggled "Oh, so sorry, *Detective* Castillo. What is it that you want me to do?" She deliberately sashayed her hips, rubbing her ass against his erection.

"Fuck, JJ. We're on the street. If you don't stop that, you'll be face down in the backseat of the SUV, and I'll be dragging those shorts over that sassy ass of yours. So behave." With that he swatted her bottom.

"Damn it, Jonas."

His chuckle was low and seductive as he took her hand and gingerly led her around the car then settled her in the passenger seat. "Behave."

Once he was in the driver's seat she turned to him. "Just where are we going? Am I even dressed appropriately for this adventure?"

"Not to worry. I had Lucia pack your bag."

JJ frowned. "Lucia? She helped you with this?"

Jonas laughed and his voice washed over her like warm chocolate. "Yep. Everyone did, even your ball buster of a boss. You have a whole week off from work."

"What? You really can't do that. I have things I need to —"

Jonas squeezed her hand. "I know you have things you need to do. But we're taking one week. Just us. Besides, don't you want me all to yourself? Imagine the things you could do to me with a blindfold and handcuffs?"

JJ opened her mouth then snapped it shut. "You do have a point."

"Somehow I thought you'd see it my way," he chuckled.

Wherever he was taking her, it took forever to get there. They were in the car a solid hour and a half. Of course it was Jonas, so it wasn't like they had nothing to talk about.

They made their list of movies to see over the next few months, where to take Isabella for their next outing. Easy stuff. The kind of stuff she never thought she'd be able to share with anyone. But she had it now. And her life was downright perfect. She couldn't have asked for anything better.

Of course, there was a part of her that was still afraid she didn't deserve this. That she didn't deserve *him*.

No. Stop it. No more self-defeating thoughts. You deserve all the happiness in the world. She had to get used to believing it. With Jonas by her side, she did.

He finally pulled the car over and squeezed her hand. "We're here, baby."

"Can I remove this now?"

"Was it that terrible? I mean, I've never brought anyone to my secret lair where I plan to chain you up and never let you go. But thanks for coming willingly."

JJ laughed. "As long as you promise to have your way with me every second of the day, I probably won't complain too much."

His chuckle was low as he reached over and undid the knot. "That can be arranged."

When the blindfold was off JJ blinked, trying to let her eyes adjust to the light. When she looked out the window, all she saw was green. They were in the woods. In front of them was a large rustic-looking cabin.

"Where are we?"

Jonas gave her a grin. "Somewhere no one will bother us. They don't have cell reception out here. Not to worry," he pulled a black bag from the backseat. "I have satellite phones in case of emergency. Out here, it's just you and me. For a whole week."

Oh wow, he'd done this for her. Except, the woods? She wasn't really a rustic kind of girl. She was more *glamping* than camping. But still, she did love the sweetness of the gesture. He wanted uninterrupted time with her. And they were going to get it. For a whole week. With no cell phone. Or TMZ. But she would survive it. Because she had Jonas, and honestly, they could be as naked as they wanted anywhere they wanted. So that was definitely a bonus.

"This is beautiful. You didn't have to do this."

"Yes. I did. Everything has been kind of a blur since we got together. I wanted to slow down, so I can show you how much I love you."

And how the hell was she supposed to not completely fall in love with him all over again?

Jonas climbed out of the car, speeding around to her side to open the door for her. "Come on. Let's have a look inside."

"Do you want to grab the bags first?"

He shook his head. "Nope. I've had a hard on since we left the city. So if you don't mind, I want to make love first. And then I can get the bags."

He practically dragged her to the front door of the cabin before unlocking it. JJ had no choice but to giggle and follow behind. When he opened the door, she gasped in surprise.

While the outside and the surroundings were completely rustic and secluded, the inside was utterly modern. Rustic-cabin modern, with glass, granite and stone. "Oh my God."

Jonas chuckled. "Woman, you think I don't know you? You'll still be able to catch up on all your shows. I'll even marathon watch *The Bachelorette* with you. But if you tell Oskar that I enjoy it, I may have to kill you."

She laughed, doing a little happy swirl as her boots clicked on the hardwood floor. "Jonas. It's gorgeous."

"You like it?"

She nodded. "I was a little worried that you were going to have me chopping wood and stuff, but this is — *Oh my God* look at the fireplace."

"Yep. I had the whole place remodeled around the fireplace."

She whirled around to meet his gaze. "What do you mean you had this place remodeled?"

"Oh you know, when I knew I couldn't stop touching you, I figured we might need a place to get away. So I started having some guys bring it up to your standards."

She rapidly swiped tears away. "You did this for me?"

He nodded. "Of course. I would do anything for you. I love you."

The warmth that spread through her chest was uncontainable. She'd never been this happy in her life. "Well, Mr. Castillo, I would like to show you my gratitude. But first, we need that blindfold."

———

JJ loved the fireplace so much that after a full tour, Jonas insisted they spend the day curled up on the couch in front of it. He'd brought along sandwiches and a bottle of wine, so they snuggled before a crackling fire, eating and just relaxing.

To anyone else, it might not seem like a huge deal but to JJ, this was the culmination of a lifelong dream. Something she'd always hoped for but never dared to dream could be possible for a mouthy blonde from Brooklyn.

Contentment.

"What are you thinking about?" Jonas murmured, nuzzling her cheek. "I've gone to a lot of trouble to put a smile on your face and I don't want anything ruining that."

She reached up to caress his face. His beard was just starting to grow in so he had that sexy scruff she absolutely loved. He was so handsome, her guy.

"You. This. How I never thought this would happen to me," she answered finally.

"What? Having your own house?" Jonas raised his eyebrows. "You're smart and driven, JJ. I know that you would have been a homeowner eventually if you wanted to be."

JJ sat up slightly. "No, not that part. I mean, yes, the house was part of the dream. But not the most important part. It was about this," she gestured between them. "I had this whole picture in my head of what my dream life would be."

"Tell me," Jonas whispered.

She closed her eyes. "I used to imagine living in a cute little house in a quiet community. Where all the neighbors know each other and say hello while getting their mail or pruning the rosebushes. I would have a big kitchen and could cook those crazy huge meals like Nonna DeMarco always does and invite lots of people. Especially the ones with no family of their own."

"That sounds beautiful, baby. Why would you think you couldn't have those things?"

She leaned forward and kissed him. "Because I haven't gotten to the most important part yet. My favorite part of the dream was when I'd imagine who I was coming home to. A man who was strong, funny, and not afraid to call me out on my shit. The kind of man that I respected and loved. Someone I loved so much that I wanted my children to be just like him. A perfect blend of the two of us."

A slow smile took over Jonas's face. "Children, huh? So there were children in this dream? How many are we talking?"

JJ chuckled. "A few. Honestly, it didn't even matter. I just wanted someone to love. Whether it's one, two, or even six, I'd be happy."

"Six?" Jonas repeated with alarm.

She had to chuckle at the look on his face. "I'm just saying. However many I had, I would count myself as lucky. I never wanted to admit it, but I've always wanted to be a mom. And I would be a good mom. I wouldn't try to force my kids to be more like me. I would love them exactly as they are."

He grinned, too. "You would be a great mom. I have no doubts. Fierce and willing to shoot and stuff in a suitcase anyone who threatened them."

JJ laughed. "You're never going to let that go are you?"

"Never. I've never been so damn mad and so damn proud at the same time."

He glanced over at her with a sly smile. "So, this perfect life you used to imagine, is that still what you want?"

JJ leaned back and stared into the flames. "Yes," she whispered. "More than anything."

Jonas carefully slipped his arm out from beneath her head

and then knelt on the carpet at her feet. "Good. Because I want to be that guy in your dream. The one you come home to every day, the one who makes you smile, and the one who loves you forever. I want to have those six kids and wave at our neighbors together."

JJ could barely speak. "Oh my god. Jonas!"

He wiped away a tear from her cheek. "I've finally taken you off guard, I see. I plan to do that a lot for the next fifty years."

She threw her arms around his neck. "You did! I can't believe you want that. Are you sure you're ready to take me on?"

Then his hand came from behind his back holding a ring, a simple round diamond on a gold band.

JJ gasped. "You have a ring? I thought you were just saying someday."

"No. I'm saying right now. Let's get married and raise hell together. I can't wait to get our life together started." He sobered, his expression more serious than any she'd ever seen him wear. "I want to give you everything, Jessica Jones. Especially my last name. Will you marry me?"

"Yes!" she squealed and pulled him close. He kissed her

softly, and JJ knew she'd never been happier than this. But of course, she couldn't resist messing with him a little.

"But about this last name business, how about you take my last name? This is a new millennium after all."

He threw his head back and laughed. "We can hyphenate both of our names, Miss Ballbuster. How does that sound?"

She grabbed him by the front of his shirt and kissed him.

"It sounds like a dream."

———

THANK YOU for reading the FORCE duet! Ready for more? Well, you guys asked for more of Blake Security... you asked for it, you got it!

Rafe's story is next and it is DEEP. Keep reading for a juicy excerpt!

AVAILABLE NOW
www.malonesquared.com/deep

AVAILABLE NOW

www.malonesquared.com/deep

Another steamy alpha romance from the NYT & USA Today bestselling authors of SHAMELESS.

She didn't just bring me back to life. She brought me back to living.

You think you know my story, but you have no idea. How could you? I cover my tracks well.

After a hellish past, I've got a good thing going being hired at Blake Security. I'm one of the good guys now...protect and serve and all that jazz.

Kicking ass and rescuing damsels in distress - all in a day's work.

Then I discover *this* damsel is not that innocent.

EXCERPT of DEEP © January 2018 M. Malone and Nana Malone

"If you're done chatting with your boyfriend, it's showtime."

Rafe pocketed his phone and rolled his eyes at his sometimes partner, Oskar Mueller, from Blake Security.

"What's the matter, sweetheart, you don't want me having anyone else to talk to? It's okay to be jealous, you know. You just have to tell me and you can have all my attention." Rafe blew the German a kiss.

It was sure to piss the guy off, but Oskar's anger was better than his asking questions Rafe wasn't ready to answer. The phone calls that wouldn't stop needed to remain his secret for now.

Oskar bared his teeth and flipped the safety off on his weapon. The two had a slightly contentious relationship, but Rafe was certain the German would come around eventually. Rafe had once tried to kill him, sure, but how long could anyone really stay mad about that?

"Whatever. Let's do this. I don't want this asshole getting away again."

Rafe nodded briskly. No one was getting away on his watch. Oskar headed north and Rafe went east, as they'd planned. The company tech guru, Matthias, had already given them the route Douchebag would be taking.

Douchebag's real name was Nathan Miller. Normally Blake Security would let the cops deal with a drug dealer, but Nathan had an interesting forced-recruitment scenario going on. He also had a history of pulling women into his schemes, women that he abused and kept against their will. *That* ticked off every single member of the team, so Rafe and Oskar had been sent to deliver a cease and desist letter of sorts.

Rafe stepped out from the alley just as Nathan rounded the corner.

Douchebag sneered even though Rafe had a good two inches on him. "Watch where you're walking, asshole."

Rafe cracked his neck even as a shot of adrenaline flooded his veins. He would never admit it out loud, but he fucking lived for this shit. "You know what? I don't think I will."

His first jab sent the guy's head snapping back.

"What the fu—"

Poor Nathan didn't get another word in because he was tasting Rafe's knuckles again. "Now, Nathan... you, me and my associate, if he ever gets here, are going to have a heart-to-heart about your business practices. And the way you treat women."

At his words, a small blond head peeked out from behind Nathan. In one smooth motion, Rafe shoved Nathan to the side and stepped in front of the girl.

"Hi, Callie. Your brother sent us."

Her eyes immediately filled with tears, but she nodded frantically.

"I don't think you know who the fuck you're dealing with," Nathan growled from behind him.

Before Nathan was even done with the sentence, Rafe had his gun in the guy's face. That shut him up pretty quickly.

"Callie, I need you to wait for us beside that Dumpster.

And close your eyes. Okay?" He didn't take his eyes off Nathan, but he listened to the soft fall of Callie's footsteps as she obeyed.

Nathan glared at him even as Oskar strolled down the opposing alleyway. When he saw Rafe's gun out, he looked pissed.

"Oh hell, you got started without me?"

"Next time don't bother to pretty yourself up for me. It's no use really. Your face is your face. And you can relax. I left plenty of ass kicking for you."

Oskar just grinned. "You're so good to me," he said as he unsheathed his knives. As his partner moved forward, Rafe walked to Callie and held out a hand to her. He led her around the corner so she wouldn't have to see what came next.

Callie flinched and peered up at Rafe from tired eyes. Her makeup had run, so there were dark smudges on her cheeks. It was a look he'd seen many times before, the universal expression of defeat. That was what it looked like when good people gave up hope.

"What happens now? Nathan will never let me go."

Rafe wasn't good at this part. The comforting, the drying

of the tears. Years ago he had been. He'd been the person who held his baby sister when she cried and told her that everything would be okay. Then he'd had to leave her, and all that emotion ceased to exist.

But this was supposed to be a new beginning, wasn't it? Going forward, he could decide what kind of man he would be.

"He *will* let you go. I'm going to make sure of it." Rafe didn't touch her, wasn't sure if it would frighten her, but he did gesture the other direction to let her know that it was safe to walk that way. They didn't need to stay; Oskar had things well in hand.

As Rafe turned to walk behind her, his skin prickled. He paused, then glanced over his shoulder. Oskar already had Nathan on the ground and was securing him with zip ties. Rafe's eyes scanned over the alley and then up to the roof of the buildings above. It was dark, and only a few of the windows in the building were lit up. Most people were asleep right now, completely unaware of the things happening floors below. People in this neighborhood didn't *want* to be aware of what was happening outside. The less you knew, the safer you were.

Rafe knew all about that.

Nathan was on the ground, no longer struggling. In about an hour, he'd be found by the police with a kilo of cocaine strapped to him and a weapon that had been used in a murder a year ago.

The gun was actually Nathan's; they hadn't manufactured that. He'd wiped it down and asked one of his runners to dispose of it. That same runner had come to Blake Security for help getting his sister away from Nathan.

"All good?" Oskar appeared at his elbow, his eyes narrowing as Rafe continued to peer at the buildings around them.

"Yeah. Just had a feeling..."

Oskar snorted. "Your Spidey sense was tingling?"

Rafe scowled. "You can never be too careful."

"You don't need to be so jumpy. You're not a narc anymore, remember? We're the good guys."

"I was never a narc," Rafe responded automatically. But as they led Callie back to the SUV they'd parked a few streets over, the other man's words rolled around in his mind.

The good guys.

What did that even mean? Fucking guys up in dark alleys, planting evidence? Not so different from his past. Except now he was the one making the decisions.

For years he'd been a member of ORUS, an elite shadow organization supporting the US government. Now he was his own man, no longer a weapon to be used for unknown agendas. He could decide what was right and what was wrong. After what they'd done, Callie would be going home and sleeping in her own bed, safe and sound. The streets of New York would have one less asshole peddling poison to those too vulnerable to protect themselves.

Messy, yes. But it was the best result they could have asked for. Rafe had learned over the years that he couldn't always make things right, but he could try to make them better.

Maybe better was enough. For now.

———

She had no idea what he was doing.

Diana Vandergraff squinted and then blinked as if her eyes were deliberately deceiving her. She watched in disbelief as her target walked away from the drug dealer, instead approaching the woman behind him. Even from a distance and through binoculars, she could see that his movements were gentle. Reassuring.

He was reassuring her? Nothing about this made sense.

Then again, nothing about Rafael DeMarco made sense. And she would know. She'd been watching him for ages now.

Stalking. You've been stalking him.

Diana smiled in satisfaction. Yes, she'd been keeping tabs on DeMarco for almost a year. It was fitting, really. The hunter becoming the prey. After all the people DeMarco had tormented, now he was the one who was looking over his shoulder.

At first she'd only tailed him to and from his apartment. Ideally, she'd have loved to get in there and look around right away, but the place was like a fortress. While posing as a pizza delivery girl coming to the wrong door, she'd noticed the steel contacts around the doorframe. Definitely not your average security system. Besides that, DeMarco rarely left the place except to go to a modified warehouse in Manhattan. The building had been demolished and rebuilt in the early 90s. The first five floors were still warehouse spaces, but a commercial building had been constructed on top of that, boasting some twenty floors. And at the very top sat a penthouse... home of Blake Security.

So far she hadn't been able to determine exactly what he did there. Either way, she wouldn't give up until she'd peeled back every layer DeMarco had. It didn't matter how long it took or that she was currently cold, cramped, and uncomfortable while spying on him from a rooftop.

It had been too long, and she'd come too far to give up now.

Movement below caught her eye, and she swung the binoculars toward the blond giant Rafe had met up with earlier.

Oskar Mueller. German. Employed by Blake Security for five years. Master's degrees in finance and economics. Employment history blank for years until he started working for Blake Security.

Her mind ran through all the available data she'd uncovered on Mueller. Information was hard to come by on everyone employed by Blake Security. Something she was sure was deliberate. But she'd been able to find out the basics from a routine background check.

Mueller was currently roughing up the drug dealer and finally dropped him with one punch to the face. Diana winced. Not that she felt any sympathy. The guy was clearly not a Cub Scout leader. Everything she'd uncovered led her to believe the firm had a great reputation.

Which didn't explain why the hell they'd employ a known killer like DeMarco.

Her fingers tightened around the binoculars. Hatred was a powerful drug, and for years she'd been fueled on a steady diet of it for the man who'd killed her father. He was her personal bogeyman and the personification of everything evil in this world. Rafael DeMarco was the very thing that tormented her dreams.

"Deep breaths, Diana. Deep breaths," she whispered to herself, closing her eyes briefly to bring her emotional reaction under control. Emotions weren't something she allowed herself to indulge anymore. They only got in the way. The last person she'd loved, truly loved, had been murdered right in front of her, and she'd been haunted by the loss ever since. There was room in her life now for only one thing, and it wasn't love.

It was vengeance.

Her eyes popped open at the sounds below. Mueller had

finished with the now-unconscious man in the alley, and DeMarco was still talking to the woman. Part of her wanted to stand up and scream, warning the other woman.

Don't trust him.

He's not as he appears.

DeMarco had taken away the last person who loved her, and for what? Money? Diana ached at the thought that her father had suffered because he was trying to protect her legacy. The Jewel of the Sea had been the only thing left of her mother, and it had been willed to Diana. No doubt her father had received many offers to buy it after her mother's death, but he'd always told her that he would protect it for her until she grew up.

He'd never had the chance to keep that promise.

Diana adjusted slightly, moving her leg to stop it from cramping. The wind blew a harsh caress against her exposed cheek, and she tugged the black knit cap covering her hair lower. DeMarco was still talking to the woman. What could he be saying that would take this long? But there was no denying the difference in his body language when talking to the woman versus the guy in the alley or Mueller.

Diana smiled as ideas sprang to her mind. For the past year, she'd laid the groundwork to take DeMarco down to the best of her ability, even establishing a fake lease and utilities under an alias. All it had taken was paying the right people at the right times. But none of it meant anything if she couldn't get close to him.

But it appeared that big, bad DeMarco had a weakness.

"So you have a knight-in-shining-armor complex, huh? I can use that."

Just then DeMarco paused and glanced up and over his shoulder. It shouldn't have caused any reaction after all this time, but she thought again how wrong it was that he would be handsome. But wasn't that always the way of things? From this distance, she couldn't make out the expression on his face, but Diana got a quick impression of impatience and suspicion before she ducked down behind the brick barrier of the roof.

There was no way he could have seen her from such a distance, right? Despite all the reports she'd read to the contrary, Rafael DeMarco wasn't superhuman. He was fallible just like all of them. Blood and bone. He would bleed red just like anyone else.

And just like any other man, he couldn't resist a damsel in distress.

Diana stood slowly and then peered over the ledge again. The alley below was empty save for the still body of the drug dealer. She needed to get out of here. Even in this neighborhood, a body drew heat. Attention she couldn't afford right now.

After all, she had a plan to execute. She smiled to herself before gathering her equipment.

"One damsel, coming right up."

AVAILABLE NOW

www.malonesquared.com/deep

M. MALONE is a 2019 RITA® Award winner and a NYT & USA Today Bestselling author of completely inappropriate romantic comedy. She spends most days wearing Wonder Woman leggings and T-shirts that she's embarrassed for anyone to see while she plays with her imaginary friends.

She lives with her husband and their two sons in the picturesque mountains of Northern Virginia even though she is afraid of insects, birds, butterflies and other humans.

She also holds a Master's degree in Business from a prestigious college that would no doubt be scandalized at how she's using her expensive education. **minxmalone.com**

USA Today Bestselling Author, **NANA MALONE**'s love of all things romance and adventure started with a tattered romantic suspense she borrowed from her cousin on a sultry summer afternoon in Ghana at a precocious thirteen. She's been in love with kick butt heroines ever since.

With her overactive imagination, and channeling her inner Buffy, it was only a matter a time before she started creating her own characters. Waiting for her chance at a job as a ninja assassin, Nana, meantime works out her drama, passion and sass with fictional characters every bit as sassy and kick butt as she thinks she is. **nanamaloneromance.net**